The Piper's Tune

Stephen Edden

Lowdham 2014

The Piper's Tune

STEPHEN EDDEN

1 3 5 7 9 10 8 6 4 2

First published 2014 by DB Publishing, an imprint of JMD Media Ltd, Nottingham, United Kingdom.

ISBN 9781780911632

Copyright © Stephen Edden 2014.

The right of Stephen Edden to be identified as the author of this work has been asserted by him in accordance with the Copyright, Designs and Patents Act 1988.

All rights reserved. No part of this publication may be reproduced, stored in or introduced into a retrieval system, or transmitted, in any form, or by any means (electronic, mechanical, photocopying, recording or otherwise) without the prior written permission of the publisher. Any person who does any unauthorised act in relation to this publication may be liable to criminal prosecution and civil claims for damages.

A catalogue reference for this book is available from the British Library.

Printed and bound by Copytech (UK) Limited, Peterborough.

For C.A.H

This is Perty's story.

In 1135, her surviving kin included:
her grandparents,
Grandfather Aart and Grandmother Edie,
their children – Wilburh, Osbert and Sunny –
and the offspring of these three.

Aunt Wilburh was married to Uncle Talbot.
Cousin Robin was their son.

Uncle Osbert had neither a wife nor any children.

Sunny had two children in his care: Eadwerd and Perty.

Part One

HEAD

I

Uncle Osbert entered the room wearing his usual look of disdain. He stood there for a moment, while he became accustomed to the sudden dearth of sunlight. But then his eyes softened – almost imperceptibly – as they alighted on me.

'Hello, Ossie,' Grandmother Edie greeted him.

He nodded.

'Let me get straight to the point,' he began. 'The firstborn son of the late Seigneur is of the opinion that I, his Overseer of the Works, should find a wife. I therefore propose that Perty and I should be wed. She has a bright mind and, with further guidance on my part, she would become an asset to me, particularly since she's ripe for child-bearing, notwithstanding the issues over her own birth.'

For a few awkward moments there was silence. It took a lot to shut my father and the others up. But Osbert – a man in his mid-forties – had just proposed marriage to his brother's daughter. Me.

In Osbert's defence, I should point out that he's a foundling, not strictly a blood-relative. His origins are rarely spoken of. Grandmother Edie insists on this. She makes it clear that her children – Wilburh, Osbert and Sunny – are loved in equal measure.

Nevertheless, I didn't know how to respond.

I saw Aunt Wilburh shake her head in disbelief as she stirred the pottage, heating over the fire. Her husband, Talbot – lying asleep, slumped against the wall – snorted, as some sprite or other troubled his dreams.

'Well,' Grandmother Edie said.

'Well, well,' Grandfather Aart added.

Osbert coughed, before continuing.

'While you ponder my proposal, Perty, you might think on this. Firstly, that you'd be living with me in my quarters which, whilst modest, are safe in the castle grounds. Secondly, that, in stark contrast to your feckless father, I, Osbert, am feckful. Yes, Perty. The man who proposes to you is a man who effects change. He wallows neither in squalor nor the past. Unlike your father, Sunny, who sits there, piping his nonsense on that infernal whistle. Or, indeed, your Uncle Talbot, who's a man of few deeds and copious amounts of indolence.'

Another pregnant silence. He had a point.

'Well, I'll be off then. I have things to do. Changes to effect and decisions to come to. I would suggest that, rather than responding with haste, you ponder the matter for five days, Perty. I await your answer with considerable interest.'

'No pottage, Ossie?' Aunt Wilburh asked, but my uncle seemed not to hear her, as he left.

Sunny exhaled sharply into his whistle. Not a pleasant noise.

'I've absolutely no idea what goes on in that man's head,' he said.

Grandfather Aart and I watched as Uncle Osbert aimed a half-hearted kick at the cur who dogged his tracks and who'd been waiting patiently outside for him. The cur backed away, warily, but he wasn't going to give up on Osbert just yet. Curs know when someone needs to be shown how to love.

Grandfather Aart says that for as long as there are people, there'll be curs.

'Even in those terrible, terrible years, when there was no food. Nothing. When misery was heaped on misery. When we had to chew on strips of old leather to keep the hunger pangs at bay. After all the vermin and the cats had been eaten. Even then, we slaughtered the curs with a heavy heart,' he says.

The English and their love of curs, Sunny joins in. It's because we Anglo-Saxon scum and the curs both share an understanding of suffering, of being ordered about. Being told where to sit and where we can and can't run. Of having to please our masters when we can barely comprehend what they're trying to tell us. Of being beaten for wrongdoing – having unwittingly displeased our betters – when we're trying to do our best.

In short: we're both accustomed to being barked at. We're flesh to be beaten or otherwise abused. We're there to serve, without complaint. This, and this alone, is what our Norman overlords call our *raison d'être*.

Uncle Osbert had aimed a kick at the cur. Because, when a man's kicked hard enough and often enough, he'll either crawl into a corner or he'll find someone or something else to lash out at.

The cur, deftly averting the blow, was unshaken. He looked up at Osbert with that mixture of awe and love.

As Osbert and the cur disappeared from view, Sunny placed the whistle to his lips again, piped a tune and then, finally, spoke up.

'Did you hear that, Perty?' he asked.

'Yes,' I said.

'And what did you hear?'

'Notes, father. Some were beautiful. Others less so.'

'Not the words?' he sighed. 'Why will the whistle only ever speak to me?'

It had talked about love, Sunny said. The whistle had said there are those who love with their heads. These are the men who'll select a wife on the basis of her usefulness. There are those who love with their lips. From such men, words tumble easily. They have what we call *the gift of the gab*. Finally, there are those who love with their hearts.

'Men and boys will come knocking at your door, Perty. And you must choose how you'll love and be loved. As for me, I love you with all three. With my head, my lips and my heart. And that's how it should be with a father and his daughter.'

'What does the whistle tell you my answer to Uncle Osbert should be?' I asked.

'The right one,' Sunny replied, unhelpfully.

'Thank you for that advice,' I said.

'The whistle also says you're an extraordinarily bright young girl, capable of making her own decisions without the help of a clapped out wooden pipe,' he said.

The pottage was ready.

Inspired by Grandfather Aart's talk of kicking and curs, Aunt Wilburh instructed her only surviving son – my cousin Robin – to do the same to Uncle Talbot.

'Wassat?' Talbot muttered, looking up.

'Food,' Wilburh informed him. 'Your second favourite thing, after sleep.'

'Ah, the stench of week-old pottage,' Talbot observed. 'Rarely fails to raise a man from his slumbers. You'll not believe the dream I've just been having. You don't know what you're all missing, by staying awake.'

'Uncle Osbert's just proposed to Perty,' Robin announced to his father, excitedly.

Talbot yawned, taking the news in his stride. Then he winked at me.

'I wondered if he might,' he said.

'Well, you could have warned us all,' Wilburh scolded him. 'Snippets of gossip and conjecture should be shared around to the benefit and enjoyment of many.'

'In this respect, gossip is like your delicious pottage, my love,' Talbot said. Then he turned to me. 'So what did you tell him, Perty?'

'I don't think Perty said much,' Sunny explained. 'I think she was rendered as speechless as the rest of us.'

'Excellent,' Talbot said. 'Keep them guessing, Perty. That's how I reeled Wilburh in.'

'As I recall it, I reeled Talbot in,' Aunt Wilburh said. 'Though I regard it as the least successful fishing expedition of my life.'

Talbot was standing beside her now, stretching his arms and yawning again. Wilburh pushed him aside as she carried the steaming cauldron over and laid it in front of us all.

Grandfather Aart uttered a few words of thanks to the Almighty. As one, we dunked pieces of dried bread into the stew. Uncle Osbert always bore his look of faint disgust and contempt as we tucked in. Today, of course, he'd not deigned to join us.

I have five days to ponder my uncle's proposal. Five days to mull over the reasons as to why I should or shouldn't be wedded to him. I'm not some simpering girl who'll be swept off her feet by the thought of all the comfort that marriage to Osbert would afford me. Nor am I so shallow that I'd dismiss the idea simply because he's not as at ease with himself or with the world as most men.

For all his oddity, Osbert's my uncle, and because of that I love him. But could I ever love him as a wife should love her husband?

He has the quiet wisdom of a man of more than forty years. But that seems so very old.

He rarely speaks, unless – as tonight – there's a purpose in so doing. A husband who only speaks when he has good reason to. Some might consider such a man to be the best sort of spouse. But wouldn't the long silences be stifling?

If I moved into his quarters, I'd be free of this crowded home I share with the rest of our family; with my grandparents, my other uncle and my aunt, my cousin, my father and my brother, Eadwerd, whom you'll meet soon enough. But if I left home, I'd miss them all so much.

There's no easy answer. Which is perhaps why even the whistle is, for once, quietly mulling things over. I, likewise, shall give the matter the consideration it deserves. Five days' worth of deliberation.

II

Stories grow on family trees. So says my father, Sunngifu. He'd talk all night if we were to let him, but claims his fingers are ill-suited to scribing. They prefer to dance on that wooden pipe of his, teasing stories and melody from it. The scribing falls to me.

'My ancestors had itchy feet that refused to settle in one place, but walked this land telling tales. I, on the other hand, have itchy fingers,' he says.

Sunny's a storyteller. Some would say a fool. Others – more politely – a *jongleur*. Osbert describes his brother as a wastrel.

'Do people really pay to hear your nonsense?' he always scoffs in disbelief.

Sunny insists it's a gift that Osbert couldn't possibly comprehend.

'You lack imagination, Ossie,' he says. 'Facts are dull. They're the uninteresting outline on which stories must be painted.'

Osbert invariably shakes his head.

'If you ever painted over my neat ledgers, I'd snap that infernal whistle in two,' he says.

Sunny and the whistle have always been inseparable. Were it to be destroyed, Sunny's heart would be broken irreparably. Osbert knows this.

Grandfather Aart tells the story of how Sunny, four years old at the time, had been seated on his knee.

'Whistle,' Sunny had demanded.

'Very well,' Aart had said, placing to his lips the very same, battered old whistle that Sunny still elicits music and tales from, though Aart had never quite mastered the instrument. He'd intended to call up some merry jig for his four-year-old son. But unpleasant, discordant notes had emerged, blinking, into the room.

'The whistle says you cannot be its master. It says it wishes me to take command,' Sunny said, earnestly.

'Look me in the eyes, Sunny. Are you telling the truth? Not jesting with me?'

'No, father. This is what the whistle said.'

Aart had handed the instrument to his young son.

'And *what* notes he drew from the thing,' Aart recalls. 'The whistle was finally singing for sheer joy.'

Aart had known, there and then, that the wooden pipe and the stories it harboured would be safe in Sunny's possession, safer than they would have been in Aart's own hands. Given new life by Sunny's storyteller's lips.

III

Sunny says stories are as various as people. Tall stories. Short stories. The funny and the sad. The po-faced and the tongue-in-cheek. The long-winded and the breathless. Some meandering and others as straight to the point as a shot arrow. They all have their place.

Sunny's always been blessed with the nose, the eyes and the ears for a story, knows where to look, where to sniff, where to put his snout and scratch around. The seamier places are the best ones. And although he often claims that the whistle affords him glimpses of what future awaits us, the past is a rewarding place to root up tales, too.

Sunny and I and just about everybody else are agreed on one thing. It's best if a story has a beginning, a middle and an end. True of people and their lives, too. A life without a beginning cannot be. A life without end would be eternally dull. And the middle? You want it to be packed to bursting with laughter and love. You never want it to be middling.

I ask my father to begin at the beginning. He tells me that Grandfather Aart is Grandmother Edie's beginning, and she his.

I look up and see my aged grandparents. Grandfather Aart is tall and willowy. His hair's white now and his face hollowed by the years, but his eyes still shine brightly. Grandmother Edie still moves with delicate grace, though more slowly these days. There's still joy and love in her eyes, too. Old age bestows us with a more ample helping of the virtues and vices of our youth. So says Sunny. When the energy and vibrancy of our younger selves has been slowly eroded away, old age reveals the underlying truth. The lovely become lovelier. The irascible become grouchier. When an old person's memory and strength and health have flown, look into their eyes. There you'll see the truth. So says Sunny. Grandfather Aart's and Grandmother Edie's weary eyes still sparkle with love.

They'd grown up together within the grounds of Exeter Cathedral. Both orphaned. But both safe from the carnage and devastation that ravaged England in the years following Duke William of Normandy's conquest.

Ah, yes, says Sunny. We are the vanquished, and William the Conqueror was, without doubt, the biggest *vainqueur* who ever walked this earth.

Aart had lost his mother and father to illness, exhaustion and starvation such as only the poorest can know. They'd left him in the care of the church. There were whispers that Edie – with her delicate frame and undoubted grace – must be the daughter of an unwed noblewoman. But it wasn't high-birth or her elfin figure that had drawn Aart to Edie. Joy had burst from her in a smile that spread from her mouth to her eyes and filled the room. Unbridled, undiluted, unconfined joy can have a boy quaking in his shoes.

Aart recalls the time when, fearing that a fellow-orphan might be a rival for Edie's affections, he'd laid down a challenge to climb higher up the tallest tree in the orchard.

'Yes, I know,' he concedes, when Edie shakes her head. 'It was only an apple tree, but it seemed much bigger, back then.'

The other lad had proved more of a leg-breaker than a heart-breaker, when he'd slipped and fallen.

'His prize was a broken leg and a life of being pitied. My prizes were Edie and a painful birching,' Grandfather Aart joked.

The tutor had enjoyed the birching rather more than Aart had.

'Embrace your suffering, Aart,' he'd panted. 'See how it draws you closer, with each lash across those taut buttocks, to Him, who suffered on the cross and who alone can intercede with the Almighty.'

The sin of tree-climbing was, in the end, deemed worthy of a mere ten lashes, though Aart had not felt that it had brought him closer to the Redeemer, in the way that, say, prayer might have done.

'Ah, but it brought you closer to me,' Edie reminded him.

Aart's thoughts had indeed evolved into something more heartfelt than mere friendship.

'I have feelings for a novice nun,' he'd confessed to his guardian.

He'd felt a surge of relief at having spoken openly of his love. Though the feeling of elation was as nothing when compared to the dizzying taste of his first kiss. Once you've kissed a girl and tasted not just her lips, but you've imbibed Love itself, there's no turning back. Having climbed an apple tree in search of love, Aart would be obliged to climb a mountain (in the forbidding form of the abbess, who didn't take too kindly to declarations of love for her novice nuns by lusty young lads).

Osbert doesn't understand any of this, says Sunny.

'Heartfelt declarations of love fall outside my purlieu,' he intones, cruelly impersonating his brother.

Osbert keeps everything locked up. His fears, his hopes. Most of all, any hint of love. But love can't stay imprisoned. It's a living thing, not a treasure to be hoarded. Gold can remain untarnished, undiminished in the dark. Brought back into the light it glisters as soon as the light dances on it. But love is more akin to a plant. Starved of warmth or light, it will surely wither and die.

Would I be able to help my Uncle Osbert to set himself free? Or would I become a prisoner in my own new home in the castle grounds, protected from the sting of penury, but cocooned from joy and light and warmth and unbridled love?

I've reason to be grateful to Osbert, because he taught me to read and write. But whether or not I should see this as grounds to marry him is what vexes me. I need neither Sunny nor his whistle to remind me how fearfully cold and miserable it was, having to sit there in Uncle Osbert's quarters. My brother Eadwerd, my cousin Robin and I.

A castle room is blessed with stone walls that keep out the rain and withstand fire. But they can't keep out the cold and Osbert has always been too busy, too distracted or too parsimonious to light a fire. My uncle and my father couldn't be more different. Where Osbert measures success – *betterment*, as he calls it – in pennies possessed, Sunny's currency is happiness.

My happy-go-lucky father, Sunngifu, shrugs his shoulders and asks why we should ever wish to fight life, when life is mightier than us. Life was there long before we were and it will outlive us. If you're going to fight someone or something, he says, then either pick on someone your own size or (preferably) choose somebody smaller than you. Take life as it comes, he says. For every uprising there's a downfall, for every upside, a down, for every upstanding, righteous man, there's a downcast sinner. For every uplifting burst of sunshine, there's a downpour. And so it goes on. He advises me to greet all ups and downs as one and the same. There's some sort of logic and direction to my father's ramblings. We call this *phlegmatism*, he says. Osbert calls it *fatalism*.

'This was all your stupid idea,' I recall my brother Eadwerd whispering, as we sat, shivering in Osbert's room. It overlooked the shaded castle yard, though the window was too high and too small to shed any light on what was going on outside.

Eadwerd was correct.

So how had the seed of the idea been sown? Uncle Osbert had been stressing the virtues of reading and writing. Sunny had been unconvinced.

'Can't say I've ever had cause to use them,' he'd said. 'Look at Talbot, too. He can neither read nor write.'

Talbot had been slumped against the wall, as he so often was, and snoring.

'Indeed,' Uncle Osbert had said. 'Take a very good look at Talbot.'

'You make a telling observation, Ossie,' Sunny had conceded.

'Could you teach Robin and Eadwerd and me?' I'd asked. I must have been ten or eleven at the time.

'A fine idea, Perty,' Osbert had agreed. 'God has willed it that a woman must serve her master at home but I don't suppose much harm can come of it if you sit there while I teach your brother and cousin for an hour a day.'

My brother, Eadwerd, has mastered carving better than he ever did scribing. He's an apprentice now. His mason, who happens to be Uncle Talbot, says he has high hopes for Ed. By contrast, Talbot says he has only low hopes for his son, Robin. I'm a young woman now and therefore the only hopes entertained on my behalf are that I might find a suitable husband, even though I've mastered grammar and spelling far more successfully than either my brother or my cousin.

'Yours is the finest handwriting of any of my young charges,' Osbert has noted. Given that there are only three of us, that Ed writes as if his pen has the palsy and Cousin Robin is as slow as a toad in winter, this is hardly flattering.

I remember our first lesson clearly. Before we began, we were instructed to wash our hands. Uncle Osbert was and still is particular about hands being washed. We must scrub uncleanliness from the skin, he says, as surely as the penitent sinner must bare his soul to the Almighty in order to be cleansed of corrupting vice.

'Do any of you know what separates a scribe from the common man?' he asked us.

We shook our heads, fearing that we might incur our uncle's

wrath by venturing an incorrect answer. Sometimes it's best to shrink into the shadows and let others venture ideas. Ideas are like animals: harder to slay if they remain hidden in the undergrowth, easiest to kill when they first come stumbling into the sunlight.

So, what is it that sets a scribe apart?

'Washed hands,' Uncle Osbert informed us.

'What about being able to read and write?' I asked him.

'Well, yes. Maybe that, too,' he agreed. His right eye had started trembling. 'Though I'd be grateful if you'd not attempt to undermine me, Perty.'

I wasn't trying to.

He placed a copy of one of his ledgers in front of us and pointed to the letter A. Then he made us trace it with our newly-washed fingers.

When it was Ed's turn, Osbert gasped in horror. Ed had used his wrong hand.

'No, Eadwerd,' he said, his right eye trembling again. 'Use your correct hand. A left hand does the devil's bidding. We call it our sinister hand, our gauche or gawky hand. We must be resolute in this matter. There's sin in the sinister, right in the right hand.'

On the basis that my hands were cleanest, Osbert asked me to study his ledger and work through it until I'd found another A.

'Fear not,' he said. 'Although my ledgers contain confidential matters of the utmost import, their meaning will elude you.'

Thus began a journey of sorts. A voyage of discovery every bit as exciting as a trek to some unknown land must be.

Father asked Ed, after that first lesson, what Osbert had taught us.

'He learned us that we mustn't use our sinister hands and that Perty's best at washing them,' Ed replied.

'Bunkum,' Sunny said.

Sunny's inspired by a lived life and laughed laughter, the sung song and the spun story. None of these things should be constrained. Lessons with Sunny would have been a joy, but I doubt that we'd have ever got beyond the letter A. There's something to be said for order. And for washed hands, too.

IV

Uncle Osbert taught me to read and write, but it fell to others – Sunny, Grandfather Aart, Grandmother Edie – to teach me about love. They taught me by the way they held me. They told me through their stories.

'What's the truth about you and Grandmother Edie? How were you sure she was the one for you?' I ask Grandfather Aart.

'I always try to seek the truth, Perty,' he says. 'But in this matter, as in so many others, Truth just shrugs its shoulders and tells me love is whatever I wish it to be. Truth taps its temple. "It's in here," it says. Belief is as any man-made thing. As roughly-hewn or as finely-wrought as you can be bothered to make it. What truths do I believe in? Some of us believe in *God*. Others believe in *me, myself, I*. Each time I looked into Edie's eyes, I believed only in *her* and *us*.'

Grandfather Aart recounts how joy poured from Edie. She anointed him with her own joy. The abbess, whose decision it was to release Edie from her cloistered life and into Aart's arms, had perhaps been moved by stirred memories of how, when she herself was a novice, some young monk had conjured longing in her.

'Think hard, you two,' she'd said, as they'd stood before her, their heads bowed. 'Requited love comes at a price. The gentle melancholy of unspoken love, the satisfaction of self-denial and a silent, contemplative life of prayer. These all have a quiet beauty. The rough and tumble of a hard-lived life brings happiness and sadness in equal measure. It's not for delicate souls.'

The abbess knew that some things benefit from being confined. Peace, prayer and devotion all thrive in a quiet place. But joy can't be contained by four walls. Joy must be set free.

Grandfather Aart's and Grandmother Edie's first lodgings were only a short walk from the cathedral buildings but a world apart. No more than a one-roomed hovel, an insubstantial timber-framed structure, daubed and wattled, and crowned with a roof that leaked almost as much water as it withstood. Though not enough to dampen their spirits. It was dark, but lit up by Edie's joy.

'You've chosen well, leaving that place,' their new landlord had said, nodding in the direction of the cathedral. 'If a man or woman lives too long in comfort he loses his zest for life. Embrace hardship. Let squalor be your bosom friend.'

Aart glanced through the doorway, to the bustling, foul-smelling street. A different view of the world to the abbess's.

'Pimp,' the man said, shaking their hands. Edie winced, her frail hands never having been crushed in this way before.

Pimp then offered them a by no means brief summary of his life story.

He was the fifth son of a shepherd and shepherdess from the northern lakes, he explained. What his parents could boast in shepherding skills they lacked in creativity, and so they named their sons one to five, the way shepherds do:

Yan. Tan. Tethera. Methera. Pimp.

They'd liked to keep life simple. They'd counted their sons home at night. Counted out their five bowls of broth – morning and night – just as if they were counting sheep into the pen. The father and mother hadn't said much, apart from when they were counting out numbers. No stories. Why tell stories? You don't want to go cluttering your mind with such things, when all you need to know is wrapped up in your woolly sheep: their health, their girth and how many they number. They'd been of the view that stories can't feed you in the same way a mutton stew or a shoulder of lamb can. Although Sunny – he who scrapes a living as a story-weaver (or jongleur or fool) – begs to differ. What's certainly true is that stories feed your imagination and a fed imagination is a worrisome thing for a family of shepherds living in isolation on the fells, where winds howl like the long-gone dead.

Perhaps they'd not expected all five of their sons to survive to adulthood. They'd not counted on the robust constitutions of their lads: a rare error in their calculations. There was only ever going to be enough work for three of them at most. The three eldest brothers - Yan, Tan and Tethera - were happy enough to be spared the fearsome prospect of choice. To bend their heads into the wind and rain and get on with the only life they knew.

Methera and Pimp racked their brains, hoping that some idea would spring to mind: perhaps in the way a week-old lamb will be standing there and leap unexpectedly into the air because its legs have temporarily taken matters in hand and decided to push off. Methera in fact only ever had one idea, and that was to leave the godforsaken hills – fit only for sheep and not people – at the earliest possible opportunity. He made his break for freedom when, one sultry night, he met a woman whose morals were as loose as the dress that hung precariously from her. She smelt of strong ale and lavender.

Methera had helped drive the sheep to market. Sheep should be driven, not thrashed, as some would thrash a cur, a wife or a child. You must nudge them into being where you wish them to be. In short, a man ensures a sheep reaches the correct destination or conclusion, the way a wife does a husband.

(Sunny winks at me as he says this.)

Being what we term *surplus to requirements*, Methera, who'd earned a penny or two for his efforts as a drover, needed no second invitation into the woman's bed. It was a thick mat of straw, covered with a soiled sheet of linen. It smelt less alluring than she did. Presumably, she doused herself in lavender water to mask its stench. As she'd lain back and Methera had entered her, the straw had cut painfully into his knees. The woman had shown no signs of discomfort. Presumably she drank strong ale not just to drown her disgust but also to dull the pain.

Methera felt intoxicated. Before this heady moment, his only amorous encounters had been with sheep although, being open (unlike his older brothers) to ideas, he'd been prepared to conjoin with any breed or either sex. Furthermore he'd not encountered strong ale on any lips before. A sheep's breath smells of chewed and rotting grass. And their fleece certainly doesn't give off the fragrance of lavender.

Methera seized the moment as firmly as he'd just been grasping the woman's hips. He proposed that they should become man and wife. The woman thought about it for a moment. Should she be concerned that Methera smelt like the sheep he'd lived with all those years? Should she mention that she had a past as colourful as a rainbow? Besides, she was bonded to another man. In exchange for her bed, her lavender water and strong ale and the occasional meal, she was obliged to hand over every penny she earned.

She explained the last of these objections to Methera.

'Not a problem,' Methera said.

He stood up, hitched up his leggings.

By God, did the woman smell good.

Then he helped her up, suggested she smooth down her dress and remove some of the straw from her hair. Waited while she did that. Gathered her in his arms and shaped to leave.

By God, did he smell bad.

'What about my master?' she asked.

'Forget him. He'll forget you soon enough,' Methera said.

The woman placed her arms around his broad, muscular shepherd's neck and shrugged her shoulders.

Pimp had been standing in the doorway, where he'd been waiting and watching.

'I'm off then, brother,' Methera said. 'When you get home, tell mother and father I've gone. Tell them I plan to rent a parcel of land and grow enough lavender to keep my beloved sated. We'll sell the rest to raise money for the odd glass of strong ale. Meanwhile, if you see her master, tell him to come after me if he wishes to collect his dues. We'll have a talk about how much I owe him and then I'll tear his head off with my bare hands.'

Pimp had taken note of a number of things. He counted them on his shepherd's fingers.

Yanly, he'd vowed that once the sap had started rising within him (which wouldn't be long now) he'd lie with a woman. Not a sheep.

Tanly, there was good money to be had in being master to such women.

Tetheraly, unlike this master, he'd ensure – whether by force or by dint of lock and key – that none of his girls would ever escape his clutches until he was ready to toss them aside.

Metheraly, none of his customers would ever leave without parting either with their pennies or their penises.

In short: the love of evil was the root of all Pimp's money. And such would be his fame that the role of master to slave girls such as these and the name of Pimp would become as one.

'And that,' Pimp had concluded, as he'd finished pouring out his life story for his new tenants, Aart and Edie, 'is the truth.'

A man of many vices. Though brevity wasn't among them.

Edie had sat quietly in the corner, having felt some of her joy drain from her.

V

Yes, Sunny says. Some men can drain the life-blood from the liveliest story. In this respect – and only in this respect – Osbert and Pimp were as one.

'Your Uncle Osbert could bore for his country,' Sunny jests. 'A shame we couldn't have seen off the Normans by boring them to death at Hastings. Life might have been a lot brighter for all of us. Even Ossie might have conjured up the occasional smile.'

Is it unfair, the way my father disparages his elder brother? Probably. Though it must be said that Osbert's lessons in reading and writing were as a dull as the unlit room in which they took place. The mood was only ever lightened by the cur who follows him everywhere.

The first time the dog joined us for a lesson is lodged in my memory.

'The cur has gained ingress,' Osbert noted.

'Would you like me to kick him for you, Uncle Osbert?' Robin asked, hopefully.

'If you kick him, then I'll kick you, Robin,' I said, coming to the cur's defence.

Sunny has always said we must defend the defenceless, speak up for the silent, listen out for the deaf and look after the blind. I suspect this is because he watched and saw what happened to Pimp's girls, as he was growing up.

'Enough,' Osbert said. 'Let the beast be.'

The cur had sat down beside us and had begun listening attentively to Ossie. Possessed of that look of love and awe. Not in the least bored. Unlike the rest of us.

Suddenly, he began to bark furiously. The sound of the Seigneur's firstborn's hunting horn had set him off.

'Shall I birch him?' Robin asked.

'Silence,' Osbert shouted. Robin and the cur both obeyed.

'I will not have any talk of birching,' Osbert continued. A half-hearted kick in the direction of a cur is clearly one thing. A full-blooded birching is quite another.

So why was it in order for the late Seigneur's firstborn to hunt foxes?

'God has given man dominion over the animals. God has also given the Normans dominion over the English. We must question neither the ways of the Almighty nor the ways of the late Seigneur's firstborn,' Osbert said, stiffly.

'My father says the old Seigneur was a fornicator, Uncle Osbert,' Robin announced.

'Talbot should guard his tongue,' Osbert snapped.

'What *is* a fornicator?' Robin asked.

'One who . . .' Osbert gathered his thoughts. 'One who fornicates,' he explained.

'What sort of an answer's that?'

'Ours is not to question the answers of our teachers,' Osbert said.

The dog got up and ambled over to the wall, cocked its leg and pissed.

Robin looked up hopefully.

'Yes, Robin,' Osbert said. 'You're free to strike the cur.'

The cur proved too quick for a dimwit such as my cousin.

'What did you learn from Ossie today?' Sunny asked us later.

'That we must not question the ways of the Normans and that the late Seigneur wasn't a fornicator,' Ed explained.

'Bunkum,' Sunny said.

Osbert was the only member of the family to have broken free of our home, but he visited us most nights, ready to claim his share of one of Grandmother Edie's or Aunt Wilburh's stews, though the conversations were less to his taste. He looked across and scowled at Sunny.

There's no privacy to be had in a crowded home. Privacy's more often than not the preserve of the rich, the powerful and the priestly. Where you have privacy, secrets fester. And where secrets fester, untruth grows. A family boxed in a confined space has no secrets: arguments aplenty but an abundance of truth, of saying it how it really is. Hence, such exchanges are known as *home truths*.

'You should stick to reading and writing, Ossie,' Sunny said. 'Leave the fairy tales to me.'

He picked up his whistle and piped a tune that had our feet dancing and had Osbert looking on with an expression as sour as a crab apple.

It tortured Uncle Osbert to witness such abandon. I recall, clearly, how I felt overcome with pity, and walked across, tried to take his hand.

'Dance with me, Uncle Ossie,' I said, but he pulled his hand from mine and shrank back into the shadows.

Uncle Osbert dislikes being alone in his quarters. Feels uneasy in the company of others. Fears the darkness. But clings to it because he's uncomfortable in the light. Feels isolated from his fellow men, when he's spurned their company. Feels lonely in a crowded room.

The cur, Grandmother Edie and I all understand that Osbert needs love but is hard to love. But an awareness that a man is in desperate need of love is different to thinking you should be the one to whom he's wedded.

VI

Grandfather Aart – so the story goes – had been granted enough money to last him the first month, when he'd ventured beyond the cathedral walls. He needed a job. You must be able to demonstrate rare skill if you're angling for a job worth landing. Because if yours is an easily-acquired skill, there'll be others swarming over that job, prepared to work for fewer pennies than you. Worse still, if another man thinks he can do your job as well as you can, he just might do whatever he must to wrench it from you. It's a knife-in-the-back world out there. So you need a rare skill. But it has to be one that has its uses, too.

The lads who sought work had gathered in the market place. It's where any self-respecting employer comes to find cheap labour. Some of the codgers were already looking defeated, shaping to leave before they'd even arrived. You can take only so many setbacks before your pride's borne away on the wind, all your stuffing's been knocked out of you, and all your hope has fledged. Few men want to employ another who has no hope in his eyes.

There was a hush as the Seigneur's second-born son hove into view. He was young, arrogant and chain-mailed. This last was no mere show of force: he knew that just about every man (and a fair few of the woman) in the city of Exeter would have dispatched him to the afterlife, had they been able to get away with it. Chain-mail is, of course, only one line of defence. The henchmen and spies lurking in every dark corner serve their purpose, too.

The Seigneur's second-born was about to have his pick of the crop.

The Shrike, they called him. Named after the butcher bird who impales its prey on a thorny bush, allowing their flesh to rot to tenderness before consuming them. Rumour had it that the Shrike's torture of choice was to impale any man who offended him, though he had his standards. He'd never yet run his sword through a woman, the gossipmongers admitted. For the maidens, he had another form of impaling in mind. The women he'd raped endured a slower death than the men he'd impaled. Or so it was said.

The second-born son of a Seigneur – like so many other latter-born sons – must make a choice. Between God and the Devil. The firstborn stands to inherit wealth, lands and titles aplenty. The latter-born must hope for a fortunate (though not necessarily happy) marriage or they must take matters into their own hands. If they turn to God, they might find solace in quiet contemplation. They might learn to forgive their parents for having created them: a fall-back, an afterthought, the mere after-birth. They might forgive God for making theirs an unfair world, where near-misses and might-have-beens are even crueller than hopelessness. If they turn to the Devil, some take it upon themselves to rid themselves of their elder sibling and claim their rightful dues. Others are happy just to consort with the Devil in any way they choose. To plunder whatever gratification they can.

As the Shrike's horse trotted into the square, relief replaced hopelessness on the faces of the codgers who knew they'd not a cat's chance in a hounds' kennel of being selected.

The Shrike pulled the reins of his horse sharply. The horse snorted and stamped its foot. A horse is free to express irritation, safe from the fear of being impaled. Because a fine horse is worth more than any number of Englishmen.

The Shrike then shouted something that none of the gathered men could fully understand. He rolled his eyes impatiently. For

God's sake. These simpletons had lived for more than twenty-one years under Norman rule. They'd seen off one Norman king and watched another crowned. Could they not understand a few straightforward words of Norman French?

He pressed the tip of his sword against the chest of one of the serfs at the front of the crowd.

'Comprenez-vous?' he asked the man, sharply. He was met with a look of terror.

'Répondez!' the Shrike persisted.

'Mercy,' the serf pleaded.

Why in heaven was this fool thanking him? The Shrike struck the man a blow to his side. The man staggered, grateful not to have been impaled. The Shrike's patience was wearing thin. He needed to get through to these English scum. When in an unfamiliar place, surrounded by peasants who babble in a foreign tongue, a simple rule applies. You must shout louder, perhaps a little more slowly. You must bark them into submission.

He repeated his request. Aart now managed to pick up the thread. The man was looking for a dogsbody who'd do his bidding for a pittance. In such straitened times, it was at least what they call *the first rung on the ladder*.

Aart was the first to raise his hand. Standing there, a tall young man with his fresh face and curly, wheaten hair, he caught the Shrike's eye. This boy looked as if he had the important qualities: gullibility (which made him malleable) and youth (which would lend him vitality). He also looked intelligent, which was to be welcomed.

What could he do, the Shrike demanded to know. Although schooled at the cathedral in Latin and English, Aart had picked up enough Norman French to engage in conversation.

Read and write, Aart told the Shrike; haltingly, making a bold attempt not just to put his case in the Norman tongue, but mimicking the accent, too. It had more languor, none of the staccato rhythms of his native vocabulary.

Some of the others had cottoned on and a hundred or so other arms were now raised. The Shrike pointed his sword in the direction of another young man who looked as if he shared Aart's vitality and gullibility, though not necessarily his intelligence.

The Shrike enquired as to his skills. The boy looked blankly and so Aart (being too soft-hearted for his own good) whispered the words in English.

'What skills do you have?' he muttered.

'Rare ones,' the boy piped up, shedding little light.

The Shrike rolled his eyes again. Aart explained that the Seigneur's second-born was looking for someone to do his bidding.

'Vous,' the Shrike barked at the other lad.

'You,' Aart explained.

The Shrike demanded to know why he should choose one or other of them. Aart acted as interpreter as the other boy put forward his case.

'Please tell him I'd happily somersault from the city walls and into the fosse, in order to become his dogsbody,' the boy asked of Aart. 'Say I'd swim down the River Exe and, returning through the city gates, I'd lay myself at his feet.'

The Shrike seemed impressed. So be it.

The boy elicited gasps either of admiration or incredulity as he stood facing them all, crouched and then launched himself backwards off the wall. There was something approaching concern as he took his time to emerge from the putrid water of the fosse, as we call the water channel. Then he was off. The boy had at least had the wit to ensure that, once he'd made it to the river, he'd be swimming with the flow. Not entirely stupid, then.

Interest waned as he disappeared from view.

How would Aart cap this? What will he do, once the flow of the river has borne his rival back to the feet of the Shrike? Unlike the other boy, Aart doesn't believe you should always go with the flow. Sometimes (as he'd demonstrated when he'd raised his hand, earlier) you must fight the current and thus stand out from the rest.

These thoughts occupied Aart until the boy reappeared, clambered up the bank of the Exe, ran through the city gate and collapsed, soaked and exhausted, at the feet of the Shrike. He undid some of the good by vomiting something that seemed half puke and half water at the Shrike's feet. But the Shrike had seen much worse. He raised an eyebrow in amusement.

He now demanded to know what Aart was capable of.

Aart had had enough time to craft his answer while the other boy had been swept along by the river. Another lesson there. Don't be in a rush to leap in. Take your time. Assess your rival's strengths and weaknesses.

'In half the time it takes a man to swim around the city of Exeter, I could scribe a contract that binds a man to his *maistre*. Furthermore, I can do this in flawless Latin,' Aart offered.

A good answer.

At last, the Shrike was thinking. An Englishman with whom I might even rub along, though only in the way one might rub along with one's favoured hunting hound in preference to a mongrel who stands at your door, begging for scraps.

It was easy, in this godforsaken land, to imagine that fear and loathing were the very stuff of humanity. Sometimes a chink of light finds its way into the gloom. Perhaps, just perhaps, the Shrike needed more than a servant at his side. Surrounded by all those henchmen, spies and sibling rivals, one thing he lacked in his life was a friend.

The boy was dismissed. Humiliated by the chorus of mocking laughter. When you're crushed from all sides by misery, as the men crowded in the market place were, when there's little in the way of joy to cling to, then one of the few sources of laughter is the misfortune of others.

Aart wasn't laughing, though.

'Sorry,' he said to the boy.

'À demain,' the Shrike dismissed Aart.

Tomorrow. A new dawn.

VII

'God has provided,' Aart rejoiced when he'd returned home.

God? Or was it the Devil?

The day had still barely begun, Edie having only just risen from their bed, as Aart splashed cold water against his face. The water from the communal well smelt as if death had leached into it. They caught the best of the water over in the cathedral grounds. What they didn't want, they let flow to the rest of the city, but not before they'd washed themselves and their clothes in it and then pissed and crapped into it. When you splash ice-cold, pissed-upon, crapped-into water on your face, it brings you sharply to your senses.

'My new master is the Seigneur's second-born.'

Edie looked up in alarm.

'If he were to . . . If I lost you . . .'

'We must be strong, Edie. I've made my choice. Just as I chose you over the church, and I chose being with you, in this place, over a life of comfort without you, I would choose you if I had to choose between life itself and you.'

'Me too,' Edie said. Joy flashed across her face again.

The bracing splash of cold water or the balm of warm words. Both of these can anchor you so firmly in moment that you forget, for a while, what was in the past and what the future might hold.

Modestly, Edie washed herself, scrubbed at the smell of their lovemaking that clung to her. She'd been invited – before she'd left her life of quiet devotion – to return to the cathedral grounds as often as she pleased, while she found her footing in the world beyond the cloisters. She didn't want to go back into the house of God smelling of their lovemaking.

She made her way briskly through the foul streets. It was best to keep your eyes down. In part to ensure that you remained unsullied by the seamier sights. In part to ensure that you avoided becoming mired in any crap. The human crap and the dog crap were the worst.

'Tell me,' a novice nun asked Edie, once she'd taken her place beside her. 'How is life beyond these walls?'

Edie's a welcome and regular visitor. Sits beside the other girl and embroiders while she, Edie, waits and hopes for a firstborn. What else is there for her to do? There are two things worth noting about a one-roomed, ill-lit hovel. The first is that the confined space draws the one you love closer to you. The second is that beyond cooking and tending the fire, there's not much to be done inside those walls. Particularly when you own little more than the sheet atop the bed you lie on at night and the cauldron in which you simmer stews. Sitting alone in her colourless room, her joy might slowly have drained from her and her happiness would have begun to unravel, while Aart was off, serving his master. Here, seated beside her friend, embroidering, she could stitch back the fabric of her life, thread joy into it again, add back the colour.

How was life?

'Not as I'd expected,' Edie confessed.

'Does Aart disappoint you? Does life on the outside disappoint you?'

'No and no,' Edie replied. The first was true. The second, a lie.

Edie had only lived beyond the cathedral walls for a matter of days and she'd already learned the value of untruths. When we learn to meld together truths and untruths, we learn to tell stories.

As Sunny admits: fiction is sometimes truer than truth, and truth is sometimes more unpalatable, more hurtful, and falser than fiction.

The novice nun was itching to ask Edie how carnal love felt. They both understood the love a woman can feel for the saints and for the Redeemer. But such otherworldly, unsullied devotion is as different to carnal lust as ice is to warm water. Love is love. Water is water. But both take many forms.

'Tell me, Edie,' the novice nun asked. 'Does carnal love bring joy or pain?'

Edie blushed.

'Both,' she said.

There's neither joy nor pain in embroidery. Only a sense of quiet satisfaction as the picture unfolds.

For all that they lived surrounded by squalor, Edie and Aart were among the fortunate few. They knew that much.

The man or woman who works with their head is the most blessed. Others can do their bidding. Next (and this is the best an Englishman or woman can hope for in the face of Norman oppression) come those who work with their hands. Next come those who put their back into their work. Most cursed are the ones with no work at all.

VIII

'I must away,' Sunny says, stirring himself. 'I must climb into my jongleur's clothes because there are stories to be told, pennies to be earned.'

Stories are like buildings, he says. They can't make themselves up. Each night, Sunny climbs into the outfit his mother patched together for him. Each night he gathers his thoughts, takes a deep breath and follows wherever the whistle leads him. Sometimes his services are called for at some celebration or other, and, in such cases, he takes time out to prepare what he plans to say. Tonight he'll tour some of the ale houses. These performances can be thankless. But he's never short of something to say.

Stories are like friends, he says. You must nurture them and they, in turn, will come to your aid when you need them most.

He's donned his jongleur's costume, a patchwork of materials, each of them enjoying their afterlife, having outlived their useful, everyday purpose. He scrutinises it.

'Just like the Redeemer,' he jests. 'This outfit has risen from the dead and is enjoying a prolonged afterlife.'

'You look ridiculous,' Wilburh comments. Hers is a waspish tongue, but it carries no venom. In this respect, she's like a hover fly that mimics its fearsome lookalike. For the hover fly, this is a useful form of defence. Sunny says that Wilburh's waspish tongue is a defence of sorts, too.

'Thank you, beloved sister,' he replies.

Thank you? Indeed. Sunny says the secret of successful storytelling is to make your listeners walk out feeling cleverer, more knowledgeable than when they went in. They should walk out, at the very least, with a story of their own to tell. If, in imparting your wisdom, you try to appear cleverer or smarter than they are, they'll walk away diminished by the experience. So a successful storyteller must risk being regarded as a fool. Perhaps he should even welcome it.

Sunny scratches at the congealed pieces of rotten fruit or vegetables.

The badges of his trade, he calls those stains.

'What tale tonight, Sunny?' Edie asks him.

'No idea,' Sunny says, brightly and unconcerned.

Another deep breath and he's off.

So it falls to Grandfather Aart to pick up the thread of the story.

'I might as well tell you,' he says, 'because if I don't, then Sunny will. Besides, there's not much else to do of an evening.'

There are two types of work to which a man might put his scribing skills, Grandfather Aart says. God's and the Devil's. The sacred and profane.

This rare skill of his differed from Edie's rare gift for embroidery.

'I've yet to see a single stitch that I'd call the Devil's,' Grandfather Aart says.

He admits that he's not seen the one the Conqueror's half-brother Odo commissioned after Hastings. The one they worked at Canterbury, before it was shipped off to Bayeux. A wondrous, devilish piece of embroidery, by all accounts.

But scribing. Well, a man may be bonded if he so much as marks a cross on a piece of vellum. A fool can sign his life away with two strokes of a quill feather. A scribed document can make you a fortune or break you.

One thing set Aart apart from most other scribes. It's probably what reassured the forbidding abbess that she was right to let her favourite novice nun slip from her grasp and embrace the perils of married life. It's what the Shrike saw in Aart's eyes. It was the search for Truth, wherever it lay.

Maybe. But a man can't live on Truth alone. Aart's stomach knotted as he wrote down the Shrike's latest proclamation. A house to be razed to the ground so that a new structure can be built. Already the impressive new red sandstone castle of Rougemont dominated the North West of the city, but these Normans were never satisfied.

What of the poor widow and her children whom you plan to evict, maistre?

What of them?

What of your own soul, maistre? Do you not fear damnation?

No, he feared nothing. Certainly not the wrath of God. After all, did God not grant the blessed William the Conqueror this land to rule as he wished?

'I think we've built enough churches to keep the Almighty happy, Aart. If God knows what's good for him, he'll turn a blind eye to the suffering of the odd scrawny widow and her vermin.'

The Shrike took his cue from the new king. William Rufus, third-born son of the Conqueror. A man who had no need for God. His father had been in possession of many faults, but he'd been loyal to those who'd stood by him. And no one had served the Conqueror more cravenly than the Almighty. He'd granted the Conqueror this benighted country. And the Conqueror, in return, had built the Almighty churches aplenty to reward His loyalty. Rufus, however – godless, ruthless Rufus – turned his back on God. At best, this is called *ingratitude*. At worst, it's called *asking for trouble*. The Almighty's a vengeful God, best not crossed. Turn your back on Him and who knows what might come arrowing your way?

Aart's heart sank, as he scribed his master's decree. If you focussed your eyes on the vellum and concentrated on the matter of writing that which he says you must write, you can just about lose sight of what's going on around you. But this doesn't stop it eating into your very soul, corroding you.

'Why should I worry about these filthy, stinking peasants?' the Shrike demands to know. 'Each and every day I have to put up with their stupidity and indolence. I bark at them and they just look at me blankly. However many times I slap them over their heads, they continue babbling to each other in their incomprehensible English tongue.'

'They are men and women, flesh and blood, as you are, maistre.'

'Nonsense. I need a walk to calm my frayed nerves, Aart. Have my horse fetched.'

'What are they saying?' the Shrike demanded to know, pointing his sword at two men. 'Are they plotting? Are they complaining?'

'They're discussing the weather, maistre.'

The Shrike cast Aart a look of incredulity.

'The weather? What sort of race discusses the weather, damn them?' Are you telling me the truth, Aart? Remember. I employ you to tell me the unlacquered truth. You are only one lie away from being impaled. Neither mercy nor patience are virtues of mine.'

And which *were* his virtues?

'I assure you, maistre. They're observing that, though it has rained for three days, the rain is now lighter and that the crops would benefit from a spell of warmth.'

'Rain? Crops? Who cares about such things?'

'Hungry people who lack proper shelter perhaps, maistre?'

'You tempt fate with your insolence, Aart.'

The Shrike barked at the two men. He pointed his sword skywards.

'Pluie. Après moi. Pluie,' he said.

The two men looked at him blankly.

Aart mouthed the word.

'Pluie,' the brighter of the two men repeated.

The other seemed confused. The Shrike prompted him by pointing his sword to the sky again.

'*Regn*,' the man explained to the Shrike. Rain. He offered the word more with the timidity of a question than the resolution of an answer.

Aart winced as the man took a blow to his side, staggered and fell.

'They will learn to speak properly,' the Shrike growled. 'They will learn that the blight we call *Englisc* must be eradicated.'

'Perhaps their language is all they have left, maistre,' Aart said.

'Why would anyone wish to cling to such a ridiculous language?' the Shrike cursed.

Life was straightforward for the Shrike. The English were there to provide for you and, when they'd outlived their useful purpose they could crawl out of sight and die. If their presence offended you, then it was quick and relatively painless to run them through with a sword, so long as you have enough henchmen prepared to testify in a court of law that you were provoked. Your sword speaks a language that needs no interpreter. A pointed sword says: go there. A raised sword says: beware, you've incurred my wrath. A sheathed sword, drummed upon impatiently, says: you have moments to respond or I shall impale you.

Admittedly there are one or two things a sword can't say. A sword can't discuss the weather with you, for example.

IX

Sunny's storytelling didn't go well last night. His lips tell me it did, but his eyes say otherwise.

Why does he persist with it, I want to know.

Two reasons, he says. Firstly, it's the only trade he knows and ridicule is preferable to hunger. Secondly, stories are the very breath in his lungs.

A life without stories is no life, he says.

'Someone has to stand up there and tell them, Perty.'

Sunny's storytelling. Aart's truth-seeking. They share a common thread, then. Someone has to do it.

Osbert searches neither for stories nor Truth. He seeks betterment.

The ability to close your eyes, grimace and swallow your pride, however inedible it looks, however bilious it tastes. A preparedness to ignore your conscience, even when it is screaming for your attention, waving at you to look its way. Perhaps these are necessary if you're going to better yourself. Maybe there are no rungs on the ladder to betterment. Maybe there are only other people and you must take advantage of them, trample on them, use them as a stepping stone to your own success. Perhaps betterment – like the choicest foodstuffs - is in strictly limited supply and only those who clamber upwards with most determination will feast on it, while the rest must suffer hunger pangs.

Perhaps Truth is the way to a life of penury. Generosity the road to ruin. Selflessness the stuff of simpering fools. Maybe the Galilean, who spoke of the benefits of meekness or poverty of spirit, was offering mere comfort to the oppressed, not the secrets of advancement

Osbert thinks so. He thinks the city of Exeter embodies the spirit of betterment, Sunny says. Then my father's off again. Once he picks up the scent of a story, he breaks into a run. Like a hound catching a whiff of a nearby hare.

This city was burned to ash by the Vikings in the year Nine Hundred and Ninety Nine. Most of the population thought the end of the world had come. For many of them, it had. Yet, within fifteen years, the Benedictine Abbey had reared up, a new, sandstone edifice, granted to his subjects by Cnut. They're a single-minded bunch, those Benedictines, Sunny says. The Augustinians are more inclined to roll up their sleeves, get stuck in and help the poor and needy. The Benedictines prefer to build walls so that they can live lives of quiet contemplation. The Roman Walls were rebuilt, the city revived, strong enough and healthy enough to withstand the might of William of Normandy, though not strong enough to withstand the wrath of the Conqueror's close bosom friend, the Almighty, who grabbed the city and shook it firmly with an earthquake, until it relented and fell down before him with remorse for having crossed the Almighty and his best friend. That was in One Thousand and Eighty. Shaken, it dusted itself down again. Bent on betterment, it rose again. Buildings rebuilt and the imposing Rougemont castle erected to keep its watchful eye on things. Then, just in case the Almighty had any lingering concerns about this troublesome little backwater, the cathedral church was completed in the year Eleven Hundred and Seven.

'The chimney calling the griddle soot-black,' Osbert had said imperiously, when Aart had warned his son to exercise caution if embarking on a course of bettering himself. 'This whole city's bettered itself. You bettered yourself, while others were less fortunate. Why should I not have my turn?'

'Be careful, Ossie. I've barely got beyond the bottom rung. The top is a lonely, loveless sort of place. People find it hard to love you when you're looking down on them.'

Osbert hadn't listened to his father's advice back then. Nor since.

But there was something in the accusation that Grandfather Aart had sometimes erred whilst he searched for Truth.

Sunny checks himself.

'I was recounting the history of Aart and Edie,' he says. 'My father and mother. Your grandfather and grandmother. I've been lured into the story of Exeter and my brother's feeble attempts at betterment. Allow me to get back to the matter in hand.'

Four weeks had passed. Aart's and Edie's landlord, Pimp, rubbed his chubby hands gleefully. Payment was due.

'Pimp needs assurances on the matter of rent,' he informed Aart. 'Pimp takes most unkindly to many things, but most of all to the absence of rent. The absence of rent can lead in most cases to the absence of fingers. Pimp reckons on one digit for each day the rent is overdue. After ten days, Pimp runs out of ideas and evicts his tenant. Pimp has only ever relaxed his rules on one occasion when a man with six fingers and a thumb on each hand tried Pimp's patience for a whole fortnight. Such a wretch may thereafter glean money from begging, but this isn't something your landlord would recommend. There is, of course, another option. Were you to allow your delightful wife to join Pimp's girls and enter into service, Pimp could allow you to reside here, rent free. You could continue to enjoy your conjugal rights without charge.'

Edie felt sick. She felt some of her joy seeping from her. Most of the threats during her time under the forbidding abbess had seemed idle ones. The remainder had been too awful to contemplate or too ethereal to grasp. Such as the spectre of eternal damnation.

Pimp's threat of lost fingers or – worse still – lost innocence seemed wholly real.

How much safer it would have been to have remained cocooned in the cathedral grounds.

Does Love always demand a price?

The abbess had always said it does. She'd reckoned that was why the Galilean had had to die the most agonising death imaginable. The scales must be balanced. There must always be joy and suffering in equal measure, as much pain as there is pleasure and as much regretted sin as there is redemption. Without one another, these couplings have no meaning.

'I'd rather lose a limb that sell Edie. I'd rather sell my own soul than see her come to any harm,' Aart said.

'Ah, a poet,' Pimp mocked him. 'In Pimp's experience, poetry and poverty are often bedfellows.'

'Not a poet but a scribe,' Aart said.

'In Pimp's experience, prose and penury go hand in glove.'

Must everything be yoked in these damned couplets?

'Pimp bids one impoverished scribe and his delightful wife farewell,' he added. Then he stared into Aart's eyes. 'By all means help yourself to her, tonight. But be gentle with her. She's a valuable commodity.'

Then he was off. They heard him whistling happily.

'I feel sick,' Edie said. She opened the door, leaned over the open sewer that ran down the street, and vomited.

'The Almighty will provide for us,' Aart reassured her, placing an arm around her.

Edie looked doubtfully at him.

'I love you very much,' Aart added.

She had no doubt about that.

x

These stories are a mere diversion. Perhaps if we spend our time watching or listening to the stories of other lives – past and present – it distracts us from our own life and our own mortality. So says my father.

But this truth is inescapable. I have what seems to me a life-and-death decision over the matter of being wedded to Osbert. However many stories I might recount, that particular truth refuses to budge. I might try to pretend it'll go away, but it's still there. Stories might eat up time. But, unlike time, deadlines can't be eaten up.

Here's a story. About time. Sunny told it to me when I was a child. When I hung unquestioningly on my father's every word. (Which every child does, though every child must, sooner or later, learn not to do.)

They used to measure time with grains of sand. Grains of sand are like life's niggling worries. And just like the little things that vex you in life, if you grasp them in your hands, they slip away, being of little substance. If you entrap your worries in an hour glass they have no means of escape. You watch them. Time passes. The worries all fall away, but when you look, they're still there. So you have to turn them all on their head again.

Which was perhaps what motivated King Alfred to invent the candle clock. As time passed the worries now simply melted away, until, once the candle had been reduced to a stub, they'd all evaporated.

There was, of course, a problem with Alfred's candle clock. On windy, wintry days, the flame blew out and time dragged slowly. Sometimes, when it couldn't be reignited, time stood still. Then again, on warm, summer days, your troubles all suddenly melted unexpectedly away.

Sunny explained all this. But Uncle Osbert wasn't – isn't – one for fanciful stories. He leaves that to the likes of Sunny, and their brother-in-law, Talbot.

Why, Uncle Osbert wanted to know, after his three students had decamped to his quarters, do we need to split time into hours?

Because, Robin suggested, in all earnestness, we need to know what time is *hours* and what time is *theirs*.

Time was certainly dragging that day.

Osbert will have rolled his eyes in exasperation. Then explained that time was needed so that men of God everywhere might know the appointed hours at which they should pray to the Almighty.

Prime, when men of God are first called to prayer at the rising of the sun. Then, at intervals of three hours or so, dependant on the time of year: Terce, Sexte, None, Vespers, Compline, Matins and Lauds.

'What's Ossie been boring you all with today?' Sunny will have asked us.

'We learned about Time, father. Why the Almighty gave us hours,' Ed will have said.

I suspect I'll have recited the cycle of worship and that Robin will have looked on in wonderment. Robin views facts as something you're told. He's never understood that – like proffered pennies – they should be grasped, not merely regarded in wonderment.

'Time. Puh,' Sunny will have waved his hands, dismissively. 'Why measure time? The Almighty gave us the sun to set our lives by. Hours were concocted to make slaves of us all while we work to the clock. Minutes were made to remind us how time drags while we work. And I've heard tell of something called *seconds*, which are as fleeting as a fart and use to neither man nor beast. Free yourselves from the strictures of time, children. Does a bird ask itself if it's the appointed hour to sing? Does a fox await the proper hour before settling down to a meal of succulent chicken? Do I end a story in mid flow because a candle has burned to say my time's up?'

'No,' Aunt Wilburh will have chipped in. 'He normally only stops talking once he's drenched in all that rotten food the audience throws at him. The audience never gives Sunny the time of day. They do their talking with foul-smelling fruit.'

'I'd heard tell that some of his stories are too fruity for comfort,' Grandmother Edie will have added.

'Indeed, mother,' Sunny will have responded. 'But I offer my audience a balanced diet. Those that aren't too fruity are generally meaty and a bit near the knuckle.'

There were always stories. The footloose and fact-free that Sunny allowed to tumble from his lips. The dark, gloomy tales that Talbot told. The wooden sort, constrained by fact, that Uncle Osbert told. They all have their place.

But sitting through one of Uncle Osbert's lessons was surely as boring as watching wet stone dry out. Though admittedly, every once in a while, someone breathed life into them. Never Uncle Osbert. On one occasion it was a starling, or stare.

The bird, that had been lurking in the corner, had made a botched attempt to break free and started flapping wildly about the place. Osbert's voice had gone up an octave.

'I reckon it's looking for a nest,' Eadwerd had suggested.

'Get it out of here,' Osbert had said, looking at the thing with fear and revulsion and shielding his face each time it approached him. 'Expunge it.'

'Can I expunge it violently, Uncle Osbert? Can I wring its neck?' Robin had asked.

'No, Robin. Help me, Perty,' Uncle Osbert had pleaded with me.

Suddenly he'd seemed as helpless as a child.

I'd calmed the bird, by making the others sit still as I'd cornered it, covered it with cloth, and gathered it in my hands. I think it was in shock with all that battering into things.

Then, when I'd released it, there'd been a look of shame in Uncle Osbert's eyes.

'An abomination,' he'd said.

'Not an abomination, Uncle Osbert. One of God's creatures. It was only a frit little stare,' I said.

'I care not whether it was a stare or a sparrow, Perty. The Almighty has instructed us to have dominion over the fowl of the air, not to oversee their classification,' he insisted.

'If you don't know the names of all the birds and their songs and the colours and names of all the flowers, then how can you rejoice properly in the wonders of the Almighty's creation?' I said.

Uncle Osbert had looked crossly at me, as if I were trying to trip him up.

'I could teach you their names, Uncle Osbert. Just as you've taught me letters and numbers.'

'That won't be necessary,' he'd said.

I didn't know which Uncle Osbert had feared more: the bird or the injury to his pride at being taught something by a mere girl such as me.

'Some bird been ruffling your feathers again, Ossie?' Sunny had teased Osbert, later. Then he'd played a trill on his whistle.

Osbert had scowled at him.

Sunny wasn't finished. He'd a story to tell. About Osbert and birds. About the time Osbert got into an argument with a corvid.

'It could only have happened to Ossie,' Sunny laughed and then he produced something approximating the exchange on his whistle.

Osbert had been railing at a drunk on whose shoulder a jackdaw was seated. The drunk, known only as Stink, had taken the orphaned bird into his care and the two had become inseparable. In return for scraps of food and a shoulder to perch on, the jackdaw attempted certain words and phrases. Terms of abuse were a speciality.

As Osbert had been haranguing Stink, the bird had come to its master's defence.

'Piss off,' the bird had said.

Osbert had challenged the jackdaw, who'd ignored him, having spotted a worm, on which he'd alighted.

Affronted that even a bird had spurned him, Osbert had turned to address Stink.

Stink had farted and walked rudely away. The jackdaw had flapped up onto Stink's shoulder, the worm still dangling from its beak.

'No wonder the man's only friend is a jackdaw,' Uncle Osbert had murmured as he'd recounted the tale to his family.

'You don't have *any* friends, Ossie,' Sunny had pointed out. 'And you don't have the excuse that you're always farting or that you've a foul-mouthed corvid seated on your shoulder.'

XI

But back to the story of Aart and Edie. Or at least to Sunny's version of what he claims to be the truth.

Edie couldn't sleep. Aart was snuggled up beside her. Edie imagined she could still feel Pimp's hot, spiced breath in the air of their room. No amount of seasoning can mask the stench of evil. And a man's forced smile fools no one, when his eyes betray greed.

Pimp's mother and father had counted sheep. Pimp counted silver pennies. He looked at a man or a woman and calculated their worth to him. Where some might see a pretty face, Pimp saw ten years or more of earnings. When he saw a man, he sensed the chance not for banter and friendship but some custom. And a man such as the Shrike or his ilk was not someone to have you trembling with fear, but someone to have you quaking with excitement at opportunities afforded and benefits to be grasped.

'I love you,' Aart whispered, in the darkness.

Unbeknown to Aart, there were tears in Edie's eyes. Why were the church in general and the abbess in particular so fixed in their views? Why wasn't it possible to love the Almighty and a flesh-and-blood man in equal measure, to be wedded to them both? Is the Almighty so jealous that he can't share you? Why couldn't they have lain together in the comfort of the house of God and still lived lives of service and devotion? Why was the world either as white as a bleached vellum sheet or as black as ink? And why - now - so utterly, crestfallingly black?

Pimp was lying awake, too. The newly-wed girl was lovely. If he could train her to hold on to that look of undiluted joy – even if he had to beat it back into her – then men would come flocking to her bed. Men of all shapes, sizes and classes. It didn't matter. As long as they had pennies he could relieve them of. They, in turn, would leave – every one of them – with a heart full of some of that joy of hers.

XII

'Do you understand why I tolerate you in a way I tolerate no other Englishman, Aart?' the Shrike asked.

'I believe so, maistre.'

'Then tell me.'

'Is it because you believe I scribe Latin and Norman French more faithfully than any other?'

'No, Aart. That is indeed a rare gift but you have another. Much rarer than that.'

'May I ask what that is, maistre?'

'It is that you can be trusted. I trust you, because you only ever seek the truth, Aart. You have told me, have you not, that your name means you are as an eagle, in that wretched mother tongue of yours?'

'Indeed, maistre.'

'The remnants of the Anglo-Saxon aristocracy had little to teach my father and the others blessed by the Conqueror's largesse. Your buildings are fit only to be demolished and, though your books are fine enough, who needs books, particularly those scribed in the English or Latin tongues? But at least the Anglo-Saxon scum have taught their Norman betters the art of falconry. I look into your eyes and I see what I also see in the eyes of my tamed falcon each time I remove the jess from his head. It worries me not a jot that my falcon regards me with his inscrutable gaze, because I see only truth in his eyes. His is a crueller truth than yours. He has eyes only for his prey.

His every thought is of the truth of how he might track his prey and impale it with his talons. You and I are alike in one way and one way only, Aart. We are both as eagles or falcons. I am merciless in seeking to have my own way, to meet my own ends. You are merciless in your search for Truth. You would never lie to me. Not through fear of me. I suspect those years cloistered in the cathedral grounds have rendered you inured to fear. You imagine the Almighty has time to keep his eyes on you, an insignificant mortal, a pinprick in his vast domain. And yet, you and I are in one other way opposites. We both may have the eyes of an eagle, but whereas I have the merciless heart of a bird of prey, you, Aart, have the heart of a sparrow. Your weakness is your wife. Your overriding need is to bring her happiness. Love is a weakness, Aart. You love your wife. You'll love your children, when she bears them. I live only for me, for *moi*. I will serve no other. I will not even serve God. I serve only *ma, mon*. Salvation can wait until I'm old and weak and needy.'

The Shrike believes there are two roads to salvation. The first is to lead a life of sinless penury. The second is to lead a life of unbridled sin, unencumbered by guilt, and to hope that you garner enough wealth along the way to buy your forgiveness with your last, dying breath.

'Tell me, then, Aart,' he said. 'Why is it that I see trouble in your eagle's eyes? I demand the truth.'

'I hesitate to raise it, maistre. I have not asked you for pennies because you give me succour. Though I'm clothed in coarse linen, you are my chain-mail. I walk beside your horse and you are the rest for my aching legs. You give me food to nourish me, companionship to sustain me . . .'

'Yes, yes. Enough. Flattery doesn't become you, Aart. Get to the point.'

'I have no pennies to call my own, maistre. I must pay rent by the end of the week or I shall be obliged either to lose my fingers or to sell my beloved wife, Edie.'

The Shrike waved his left hand dismissively.

'Your landlord is the odious Pimp, is he not?'

'Yes, maistre.'

'Tell Pimp this. The house and its land belong to my father. Pimp is there by our grace alone. He may rent rooms out to whomsoever he chooses, but I could cast him out at a moment's notice. Tell him that you're my *right hand man*. Tell him that, for as long as you are my scribe, your right hand is as important to me as my own sword-wielding hand. Tell Pimp that if he charges you one more penny for rent, then he does so at the cost of his life. For as long as you work for me, you will remain as his guest.'

'I thank you, maistre.'

'As for money: henceforth, I shall pay you enough to better yourself. For a start, we must buy you something more befitting than that coarse linen. My right hand man should be arrayed in silken finery. Your coarse linen reflects badly on me, Aart.'

If Pimp was angered by the news that rent and Edie were both to be denied him, then he hid his feelings well. He looked into Aart's eyes, betraying not even a flicker of resentment.

'Pimp knows he must strive to retain the favour of the Seigneur and the Seigneur's family,' he responded.

No rent. No price to be exacted. Aart's right hand in the service of a devil. Edie's right hand embroidering things for God. They'd embarked on their slow ascent from aching penury to a life in which there would be pennies in their hands.

There's something to be said for unremitting poverty, of knowing no other life. Think of the fable of the hog and the apple tree. Unable to reach the bough, groaning with ripe apples, the hog satisfies itself with the notion that they were in any case probably sour and inedible. The same applies to life, when bread and water are the only things that pass your lips.

We must all allow ourselves some measure of self-deception. Not always be slaves to fact and reason and the truth.

Facts, numbers and certainty: these are the bread and water of life. Belief, instinct, impulsiveness: these are the sweet-tasting, nourishing treats.

When the opportunity for betterment finally comes, it should perhaps be welcomed only in slow, steady increments. This is preferable to the rise and dip of changing fortune.

'I believe faith and prayer brought me into the service of my master,' Aart told Edie. 'With my faith and my prayers, he might be redeemed, in time.'

Grandfather Aart was wrong. So wrong. Contrition isn't something you can ask another man to feel on your behalf. Redemption is no respecter of purse or title.

Grandfather Aart might have hoped to maintain his delusions for a while yet. Safe in what seemed like the protecting arms of his master.

He was about to discover otherwise.

XIII

I glean most of these stories from Sunny. The occasional one from Uncle Talbot. Others from Grandfather Aart, who admits that his memory's not quite what it was.

'It's all somewhere in my head, Perty,' he says. 'Just a question of knowing where. A bit of rummaging and I manage to find what I'm looking for in the end. Mind you. Your father's memory was always about as watertight as a hessian sack, even when he was a lad.'

'My stories aren't in my head, but here,' Sunny says, holding up his ha'penny whistle. Then he puts it to his lips and plays a tune to jog Aart's memory. It sounds uncannily like a horse whinnying. One particular horse.

The Shrike's *destrier*, or war horse – a magnificent animal – regarded the English with as much contempt as its master did.

Long before we ever attempted to tame them, horses were brought into this life to be hunted, Sunny says. Thoroughbred horses are probably unaware that they're supposed to be running from the merest hint of danger, not strutting around a city putting the fear of God into peasants or charging headlong into battle. Horses should be galloping around in a herd, in a state of constant panic. No wonder they're nervous beasts, provoked by the slightest hint of the unusual.

A beggar lurched towards horse and master. Little more than skeleton and skin, he was. He raised his upturned palm. He'd done it before. On many occasions. Each time, the Shrike had ignored him. But beggars have learned to become as immune to hopelessness as they are inured to hunger, Sunny says. A beggar must never give up. Once he stops holding out his palm, he stops holding out for better times.

The horse reared, startled by the sudden movement. The Shrike leaned forward and steered it in a tight circle. Having brought it under control, he dismounted, thrust the reins at Aart. He bore a murderous look.

'The man meant no harm, maistre. I beg you.'

The Shrike drew his sword.

'No, maistre.'

The Shrike was unmoved.

Aart stepped between the two men. The horse whinnied as it felt the tug on its bridle.

'How dare you defy me,' the Shrike growled.

'Even you aren't above the law, maistre.'

'And you are my vassal. If I instruct you to testify that this . . . this *thing* attacked me, then that is what you will do.'

'No, maistre. I'll speak the truth.'

'Damn you. We're finished, you and I. I shall feed you to the dogs. Pimp shall have your wife to do with as he pleases, but not before I've impaled her.'

'I plead for your mercy, maistre.'

'You have as much chance of my mercy as this wretch has of being handed a penny.'

'I'm sorry that I've offended you, maistre. Forgive me.'

The Shrike struck Aart's side with the flat of his sword.

'Damn you,' he muttered. 'Damn your foolish obsession with the truth. Damn you for choosing to befriend this miserable beggar rather than me.'

Dismissed from the presence of his master, Aart sat on the floor of his house, his back against the mud wall, his head in his hands. Truth. Was he a fool to be so wedded to it? That beggar already had one of his unshod feet in the afterlife. It might even have been some sort of blessing for him to have been impaled on the Shrike's sword. One small lie, Aart could have told. But Truth knows no compromise. A fallen apple may taste sweet, but over time it becomes bruised and rotten. A fallen apple can no more become unfallen than a plucked maiden can become a virgin again. So it is with truth and lies. A lie can't become untold.

Aart became aware that he was being watched.

'What is it, my love?' Edie asked.

'I must seek new work tomorrow, Edie. My master has discarded me.'

Edie had been shaping to tell her husband that she believed she was pregnant. Her news could wait for a better moment.

Uncle Osbert walked into the house as Sunny was recounting this story, rekindling Grandfather Aart's forgotten past. Osbert looked careworn. The cur followed him in, despite Osbert's efforts to deny him entry.

'Let him stay, Ossie. You're both welcome,' Grandmother Edie said. 'Does he have a name yet?' she asked. She'd been pestering her son for some while now to dignify the cur with a means of address. Osbert hadn't seen the point. Was a cur not a cur?

'I thought perhaps *Docga*. Dog, for short,' Uncle Osbert replied. Something must have softened his attitude.

'Well done, Ossie,' Edie said.

'Dog? You've been giving that a lot of thought then, Ossie,' Talbot observed.

Dog looked up hopefully on hearing Talbot utter his name. Osbert scowled. He was still looking at the floor.

'I've not come to rush you, Perty,' he mumbled. 'Merely to spend some time with my family.'

When he glanced at me, there was a look of real longing in his eyes. It was only a fleeting look, before he called Dog to heel, by way of a distraction.

Dog ignored him, preferring to be fussed over by Talbot.

'Very masterful,' Sunny quipped.

'Leave him alone,' I said to my father.

Osbert's lips almost broke into a smile.

A look of wistful longing had always lain hidden behind my uncle's scowl. He'd worn it when I was a child, dandled on my grandfather's or my father's knee. Possibly being told the same stories, that still induce a contemptuous snort, though they'll have changed with every telling. Sunny can certainly never resist the temptation to embellish.

Uncle Osbert's look is one of contempt or of envy. I can't be sure. Perhaps he would like to have swung us – Robin, Eadwerd and me – in his arms as he chanted to us in Latin. Amo, Amas, Amat. I love, you love, he or she loves. Osbert know the words. He can translate them. But does he understand their meaning?

Uncle Osbert was forever scowling at Sunny, at the world, at his brother's stories. Always grimacing at the sight of any displays of playful affection. Holding no truck with laughter and lies.

'All stories are untrue,' he'd chunter. 'Facts become corroded in the telling.'

Words come into the world as pure as driven snow. But when they're manhandled and shaped into sentences, they become muddied. As for stories, Osbert reckons you shouldn't believe in them. You should trust a storyteller about as far as he can throw his voice.

'My whistle says you're talking bunkum,' Sunny would say. Then he'd blow a short, sharp shrieking sound. 'Did you hear that, Ossie?'

Most of them would be laughing. But not me.

'You're cruel to Uncle Osbert,' I'd chide my father.

'Indeed,' Sunny would say. 'Being cruel to my older brother is one of the great pleasures in life.'

Uncle Osbert would glower at him with greater intensity.

XIV

Sunny picks up the thread of the story.

Aart was standing in the market place, in need of work again. Sometimes prospective employers came up to the men and, manhandling them, inspected them as if they were cattle. It was a humiliation, but one that had to be borne. No one can live on fresh air. Not that there's even much of that in this crapped-upon, smoke-filled city where only those living in the grounds of the cathedral are familiar with the taste of purity. Even the castle courtyard is filled with the sight, sounds and smells of animals.

The men heard the Shrike's horse approaching. The nervous whinnying and the thud of his hooves on the compacted earth of the streets, every now and then the sound of a metal horseshoe on stone where the streets had been worn back to bare rock.

Aart willed himself to shrink from view. It's a known fact: a man can render himself invisible. Normally, you wait for old age to creep up on you. By then, if you're too visible, you're likely to conjure revulsion or derision in the young. (If, like the beggar, you also manage to elicit fear, you'll be in some sort of trouble.) If, when you're old, you stay quiet, keep your head down, most people will walk past you as if you aren't there. It's harder to remain unseen when you're young and beautiful. When that's the case, everyone looks your way. If, like Aart, you're blessed with youth and beauty, and Truth burns brightly in your eyes, your best hope is to lurk in the shadows.

The Shrike was in search of a new right hand man. He barked for volunteers. This time the peasants knew how to respond, even if they'd barely understood a word.

'Every hand bar mine went up,' Grandfather Aart interrupts Sunny. A slight embellishment, perhaps.

Even the young man who'd somersaulted off the city wall was waving his arms frantically, trying to grab the attention of the Seigneur's second-born. This is variously called *asking for a second chance* or *seeking a chance for redemption* or *coming back for a second helping* or *being a glutton for punishment.*

The Shrike looked around. The enthusiastic response had almost put him in a good mood, though his good moods were more of the skittish than the benign variety. He pointed to a man of middling years. It could have been any one of them. He beckoned the man with his sword. The man walked forward, looking around in disbelief that, for the first time in his life, he'd been chosen. Not picked as a last resort. The Shrike, now observing the man's right arm – broken at some stage, badly set and now useless - wondered if he'd made a mistake.

He pointed at the arm.

'An hinjury, sire.'

The Shrike rolled his eyes in exasperation.

How, he demanded to be told.

'You hinflicted it, your very good self, sire, because my presence displeased you.'

'And you're foolish enough to wish to work for me?'

'Hindeed, sire. Very foolish and even more in need of work. I'd work for the very devil himself, sire. Not that you're . . .'

The Shrike had understood the gist.

'Silence,' he said, turning away from the man. He looked up and scoured the crowd. Finally spotted Aart, shadowed by a wall.

'Viens,' he barked. He quietly cursed at having used the familiar form of address. 'Venez,' he corrected himself.

Aart walked forward, his head bowed, and stood beside the man with the useless right arm.

'This boy looks as if he might obey his master's every command, does he not?' the Shrike asked the man.

'Say *Oui*,' Aart whispered.

'Oui, sire,' the man said.

The Shrike pointed his sword at the staff a man at the front was holding. Motioned for it to be handed to the man with the useless arm. Similarly, instructed another man to hand his staff to Aart.

'Some sport,' the Shrike announced. 'Whoever beats the other into submission shall be my right hand . . .' He looked at the crippled man. 'Or my left hand man.'

Aart explained this to his rival.

Were they ready? Aart interpreted that, too.

Yes, the other man agreed.

'Oui,' Aart said, laying down his staff in front of the other, kneeling and awaiting the blows.

The man stood there, clutching the staff in his left hand, bewildered.

'Insolent peasant,' the Shrike growled, dismounting.

'Hold,' he said, handing the reins to a bystander.

Then he kicked Aart in his side. And again. He kicked Aart until he lay curled and groaning on the ground. Had this been a sporting contest, the crowd would have been cheering the victor. But this wasn't sport. There was an eerie silence.

'Have you learned your lesson yet?' the Shrike demanded to know.

'Yes, maistre,' Aart whimpered.

'What have you learned? Tell them.' He wafted his sword towards the crowd.

Aart breathed deeply.

'I've learned that the truth hurts, maistre. It hurts very much.'

The Shrike mounted his horse.

'Truth will be the death of you, so help me God. Follow me.'

Aart hauled himself to his feet, wincing.

'Sorry,' he apologised to the man with the crippled arm.

'Not a problem, lad,' the man said. 'I'll take my chances helsewhere.'

That evening, Pimp was standing in the doorway of Aart's and Edie's room.

'Your bore your beatings with great fortitude,' he praised Aart. 'This is the way it must be.'

'Why?' Edie wanted to know.

'Servants, curs and wives must be beaten,' Pimp said.

'Wives?' Edie asked.

'Indeed. Flesh is best if tenderised before being feasted on.'

'What of your own wife's feelings on the matter?' Edie wanted to know.

'Pimp has heard no complaints,' he said, 'because Pimp is lord and master of his own house.'

'Perhaps your wife is frightened to speak up. Perhaps you are no less a bully than the Seigneur's second-born,' Edie persisted.

'Is this not the true order of things? Is an Englishman not put on this earth to serve his Norman masters? Is not a woman put on this earth to serve her husband? Perhaps my tenant should learn to tame his wife, with her wagging tongue,' Pimp suggested.

Then he was off.

'What a loathsome man,' Edie said, burning with indignation.

'Sorry?' Aart asked, distractedly, wincing from his earlier beating.

'I should like to meet his wife, Nell, and tell her to stand up to him.'

'Not wise, my love. If she stands up to him he'll strike her twice as hard. The truth is he's a coward and a bully. Afraid only of the truth and of those who are stronger than he is.'

Pimp's wife, Nell, had learned the art of being neither seen nor heard. If you're the sort to be preyed upon, then merging into backgrounds is a gift to cherish. Sometimes Edie had seen Nell scurrying off, her eyes fearful and darting. She had the look of a hare about her. Unlike a horse – the Shrike's horse or any other horse – a hare's not lost sight of the fact that it's only ever a blink away from being preyed upon. Nell knew that her lot in life was to be beaten. Regularly. Even when she'd not uttered a word.

Anger is never a welcome house guest and much of Pimp's house was filled either with anger or its constant bedfellow, fear. Brutality and terror passed through the walls and into every one of the dark rooms that imprisoned Pimp's girls. Locked, until Pimp chose to unlock them. Accessed at the back by a warren of corridors, so that guests who wished not be seen might hold their heads high. At the front, Aart and Edie's lodgings and, on the other side, Pimp and Nell's rooms (for, rare among Englishmen, they were blessed not with one, but two rooms).

It was a ramshackle place, framed by timbers and with thin internal walls of daub and wattle, through which anger and fear passed readily enough, although neither could find a means of escape from the house.

Edie knew she must do something. To help Nell. To help the girls. Something more than mere words of sympathy. But she was aware that anger, like love, is an irresistible force. One that overwhelms you. Love needs someone to wrap itself around. Anger needs someone or something to crash into. A fist against a wall. A raised voice and a volley of venomous words. Or a palm struck hard across a face. Sometimes the one you thought you loved is the one who's best placed to take the blows.

Nell's lot in life was to soak up Pimp's anger. Nell, with her startled hare's eyes. She even crouched like hare, whether she was scurrying through the shadows or shaping to take her blows. Nell also had a hare-brained idea that a change of heart would overcome Pimp one day.

Didn't she love him with unwavering devotion? Pander to his every whim? Turn a blind eye when he sampled the delights of one of the girls he kept locked in their rooms? Had she ever once upbraided him when he'd lashed out at her? Did she ever fail to have his food on a platter when he needed it? (As was the case with his having two rooms, Pimp was indeed privileged in that food reached his mouth via a platter and not directly from the cauldron.)

Nell was forgetting this: that whatever a bully has – a pauper's possessions or a world of riches - he needs only one more thing. Yes, even if he's been blessed with more gifts than there are stars in the sky, he still needs just *one more thing*. He needs a victim.

'I should like to befriend Nell,' Edie sighed.

'Not wise,' Aart said. 'Trust me. I know about the folly of meddling when I should say or do nothing. Pimp isn't a man to be crossed.'

'Some bread?' Edie asked.

He tore off a piece.

'You?'

'Not hungry,' she said. 'He puts me off my food. Although . . .'

Was this the moment to tell Aart, while he was sat there, nursing his aching sides and while she was still simmering from her exchange with Pimp?

'Although?'

Aart deserved the truth. He spent enough time searching for it. Edie breathed in deeply. No secrets. Because secrets can curdle and sour the most promising of marriages.

'I should perhaps start eating for two. I believe I'm with child.'

Aart rose to his feet, embraced her. Oblivious to all pain and suffering.

'Wonderful tidings, Edie.'

He kissed her. His breath tasted of bread.

Edie was going to have her hands full. She had a new life and a new cause to occupy her now, in the shape of Nell and the girls Pimp had enslaved. The days of her cloistered, embroidery-stitching life were numbered. Once her daughter, Wilburh, came into this world, then her sons, Osbert and Sunngifu, there would only be time for stitching back together other people's lives. The lives of her husband, her children and her *causes*. Stitching together the lives of family and friends. It's what most women are obliged to spend their lives doing.

XV

Aart and Edie had dreamed of a life of undiluted truth and unfettered joy.

'Look at me now,' Grandmother Edie sighs, darning Sunny's leggings, where they've worn through. 'Stitching everything together the way a wife and mother must. And why is it always that arse of yours that wears through first, Sunny?'

Grandmother Edie turns to me: the only one of her surviving grandchildren who's a girl.

'Your father sits on his rear end, playing that pipe. The only stitching he does is patching together his tall stories. Meanwhile Ossie's knees are always the first to be darned, because he spends too many hours praying to the Almighty for something or other. Fortunately, I'm spared having to darn Talbot's leggings, because Wilbur does that for him. This is a woman's lot in life, Perty. Once we're wed, we must darn our husbands' clothing. You've been warned. Enjoy your freedom while you have it. . .'

She notices Osbert's look of consternation.

'But beware,' she adds. 'Some would say it's worse to be a spinster . . . I'm being even-handed, you see, Ossie. Telling Perty both sides of the story.'

'So what do husbands do?' I ask her.

'They're busy winning bread,' Sunny pipes up in defence of men in general.

'Some of us, being more feckful than others, bring home foodstuffs more substantial and varied than bread,' Osbert adds.

'Though I simply say this in my defence. Not to apply pressure to Perty.'

Things could have been a lot, lot worse for Grandmother Edie, of course, and she knows this. She's blessed to have a husband who still loves her as much as he ever did, though his love's evolved from something light and heady to something deeper and more thoughtful, after the best part of fifty years of wedded hardship. She's grateful, too, that he's never once struck her.

Is this how it should be, though? Should a well-loved wife such as Grandmother Edie be grateful not to have been beaten in the way Nell was? Should a wife not feel free to tell a man to go off and darn his own leggings once in a while?

It's the Normans who are to blame, of course. It's always the Normans who are to blame. It used to be the case that men and women were equal in the eyes of the law. No longer. A bunch of young men, with nothing to lose but their miserable lives, came over with William, Duke of Normandy on a promise of lands, money and everything else they wished to lay their hands on. They'd even enshrined their petty male insecurities in the notion of *primogeniture*. Who in their right mind would ever imagine it was a good idea for the firstborn son and not the firstborn daughter to rule a kingdom or run the affairs of a household? Surely everyone knew that women were much better at these things than men.

Grandmother Edie is voicing such thoughts as she and her family sit around the fire.

'You may well be right,' Grandfather Aart agrees.

Osbert snorts, derisively. He doesn't make things easy for himself.

I saw the look that washed over Sunny's face. Sunny, who always leaps to the defence of the defenceless. My father, Sunny, who ended up marrying one such person.

'I thought that tonight, I might recount Ossie's exploits at last year's ill-famed football match,' he announces provocatively.

'Must you, Sunny?' Grandmother Edie asks. 'You know how much that irks your brother.'

'Feckless and foolish and feasting, like a carrion crow, on the misfortunes of others,' Osbert snarls.

'In my experience, everyone's reassured by tales of those less fortunate than themselves, Ossie. In your case, there's the chance to ladle on a large dollop of humour, too. A good laugh and game of football recalled. That and a few pints of the finest ale are what we call an excellent *lads' night out*. I expect to be groaning under the weight of pennies earned, tonight.'

'You're as squalid as that wretched patchwork outfit you never seem to wash,' Osbert snaps.

'Stop this at once, both of you,' Grandmother Edie speaks up.

There's silence, though nothing in the way of apologies. Edie knows that Sunny has the bit between his teeth. He'll already be conjuring a new version of his tale as they sit there, eating.

Poor Osbert, she thinks. Does he deserve to be a laughing stock? I wonder the same. Another curse of being a woman. We're too sensitive for our own good.

Poor Uncle Osbert. This is broadly how the story goes.

The hay was safely gathered in, the cider quaffed, the headaches not yet vanquished: it was time for the annual game of the sport they call *football*. A violent pastime and, that year, a source of dread for Osbert. The city is divided into the clergy and the commoner sort of man. Then there's Osbert, cursed with apartness. The Shrike, who, in his youth, had refereed the annual contest with a rule of iron, had elected Osbert to oversee proceedings.

'Your eye for any transgression is unerring, Osbert. Your attention to detail is absolute.'

'But, sire, I don't understand the rules of football. I beg you to spare me this ordeal.'

'Nonsense, Osbert. The rules are straightforward. The clergy must endeavour to throw or kick the inflated pig's bladder against the East Gate . . .'

There were mumblings that the clergy were always thus favoured, but the Bishop had pointed out that it was fitting that his team should strive to kick the ball in the direction of Jerusalem.

'The other scum must try to reach the West Gate,' the Shrike continued. 'Fair means or foul may be employed. You must simply keep a record of any scores. We call them *goals*. You must also intervene if the violence puckers into something life-threatening. Otherwise there are no rules. Apart, of course, from the fact that the clergy must win. They're a vindictive bunch and, were they to lose, they'd damn you to hell. Understood?'

Osbert had been quaking in his shoes at what lay ahead.

'Would you like my whistle to lend its assistance to you, Ossie?' Sunny had asked.

'What in God's name would a referee do with a whistle?' Osbert had snapped.

'Just a thought,' Sunny had said, shrugging his shoulders.

The game had gone badly. Osbert's lack of control had been evident from the off. The ball had flown in all directions as Osbert, panting, had tried to keep up with events. Several of the higher clergy had appeared to be engaging in unacceptable brutality.

'Sorry, your reverence,' one of the commoners had apologised as he'd clattered accidentally into a priest.

'An eye for an eye and a tooth for a tooth,' his Reverence had said, bundling the wretch into the open sewer, before genuflecting.

'Foul,' Ossie had cried out. Both sides had ignored him.

There had been an hiatus, when Dog, who'd been running around excitedly, tracking Ossie's steps, had seized hold of the ball and weaved and wriggled his way between clergy and commoners alike. Ended up seated at the East Gate.

Ossie had been faced with a decision, as Dog had sat there, growling protectively, holding the ball. If Dog were to be classed as a member of one of the teams, he must surely be a commoner. And yet he had scored for the clergy. This eventuality hadn't been allowed for. There were three options. Dog must be ordained with great haste, or the goal must be disallowed, or Osbert must award the goal, disregarding any objections.

On the basis of the Shrike's prior briefing, he'd awarded it.

Not normally one given to creativity, to moments of blinding epiphany, Osbert had just invented something called an *own goal*.

Osbert had immediately been set upon by three hooligans.

Dog, forsaking the ball, had run to his beloved master's side. Abetted by some of the more well-built members of the clergy, Osbert had been wrestled free.

Never again, he'd vowed.

The game had continued until nightfall. One nil to the church.

A result. No one would be damned to hell.

Why, in all walks of life, was it always one nil to the church?

'At least we can rest easy in the knowledge that Exeter city is likely never to become renowned for its prowess at football,' Osbert had growled. 'Let us hope and pray that football is confined ere long to oblivion.'

XVI

There's a smile on Sunny's face this bright morning. Last evening's tale-telling clearly went well.

'Scapegoats,' he says, tapping the side of his nose. 'A tried and tested device to fall back on when the going gets tough. And goats don't get more scapey than your Uncle Ossie, Perty.'

On with the story, though, Sunny says. We can't let Osbert distract us. We must return to our beginnings, to Aart, Edie and their trials and tribulations.

When Wilburh came, she brought pain and joy, Sunny continues. Not just at the birth itself. A child's lot in life is to bring both pain and joy to their mother.

Aart was serving the Shrike in another part of the city, beyond the reach of Edie's anguished cries. Edie's screams grew louder as Wilburh stubbornly refused to come.

Stubbornly refusing to conform would be a pattern in Wilburh's life. The very image of her softly-spoken mother, who'd never let go if she picked up the scent of a cause.

'Stubborn, maybe. But the good sense to know a womb was a better place to be than a cold room propped against a brothel,' Aunt Wilburh jests.

Edie became aware of Nell's presence.

'Master has sent me to quieten your cries. He says they must cease or he'll be obliged to administer beatings. He says his customers are unhappy.'

'Help me,' Edie said, clutching Nell's arm. She looked into Nell's startled hare's eyes. Nell looked anxiously towards the door.

'Master didn't say I could stay,' Nell replied.

'I beg you,' Edie pleaded

'We must be quick,' Nell said.

Wilburh's crown was already visible.

'Hurry,' Edie pleaded with her unborn daughter. As Edie stifled her cries, Nell became lost in the task.

She knelt, wiping Edie's brow with a damp rag, grimacing but not attempting to pull away as Edie squeezed her arm painfully.

'Push,' Nell whispered, gently.

And then, as the head slowly emerged, she eased Wilburh from her mother, held her.

'I swear Wilburh was born smiling,' Grandmother Edie says. 'I swear she looked up, smiling, at Nell and, for a fleeting moment, Nell was at peace.'

Perhaps the Almighty gave us the pain and joy of childbirth so that we might know hell and heaven on earth.

'A quiet one,' Nell said, stating the obvious.

'Not the first time you've . . .' Edie's voice tailed off. Nell looked away. Ashamed. 'You're an angel, sent to help me,' Edie persisted.

'No,' Nell shook her head. 'A devil.'

She rose to her feet and left, hurriedly.

'I knew the truth,' Grandmother Edie says. 'One of Nell's tasks had been to deliver the babies and find someone to pass them on to. A baby can't be reared in a brothel. They're a distraction and a drain on resources.'

Then she recounts how she, too, had been taken away from someone. Maybe a highborn woman, if the rumours were true.

'I don't know whom. And then . . .' She's lost in thought for a while. 'For a child denied a mother, only love can fill the yawning gap. I was fortunate, blessed by the love of the church and then by the love of Aart and my family. As for the mother who loses her child, her best hope is that time will dull the pain.'

XVII

Nell sometimes seemed more shadow than flesh. Some leave their mark wherever they go. Pimp left the imprint of anger, and fear's heavy tread. Nell's imprint was as slight as a hare's form on the meadow. She moved stealthily along the corridors that led to the locked rooms. She knew how each of the girls responded to the sound of footprints. The new girls tautened with fear as another of Pimp's customers approached, usually with the irregular, heavy steps of a drunk. The older girls, inured to the pain and shame, and having learned to live with their disgust, listened with detached interest, familiar with each type of footstep. The tentative walk of a first-time customer, wrestling with his guilt. He would have to be flattered into believing he's brought you as much pleasure as you've granted him, because this will diminish his guilt. His shame must have dissipated by the time he walks through the door. Pimp has made it clear that a customer who doesn't pay a return visit is a customer insufficiently nurtured. A girl who fails in her duty must be punished. Pimp will take great pleasure in devising a punishment that fits the crime.

No footstep is ever welcomed. But some footsteps are less unwelcome than others. The crippled man, with the face of a gargoyle, unable to find love in the outside world, comes here to love and believe he's loved. He's gentle and appreciative. Although still a duty, lying with him is almost bearable. He understands that his girl must face away from him while they cavort. He's sensitive enough to know his gargoyle's face can only engender disgust. But he can still believe for a few heady moments that he's loved. His uneven tread engenders no fear. It elicits an intake of breath as the chosen girl composes her features.

The confident, manly strides of a Norman. These are the footsteps that engender the greatest terror. The Shrike's reputation may be the most fearsome among them, but he's no more or no less brutal than most of them. Power can shrivel a man's soul. A man without a soul sees you not as a woman but as meat on which he can feast as he chooses. He'll take his pleasure, as brutally as he cares to. Then he'll cast you aside as he might throw a chicken bone to the floor. If he has any feelings at all, these are likely to be feelings of contempt for you. You know he'll be violent. You pray that the pain he inflicts is less horrific than the last time he impaled you.

Other footsteps elicit revulsion: for example, the smooth, surreptitious steps of the crooked judge and the wayward priest who sound forth about right and wrong, though they themselves are bereft of morality. Who'll curse a woman for placing temptation in front of their pious eyes. Such men are lower than turd weevils.

As for Nell's footsteps, they're as light as light itself. They barely touch the floor.

Silence can be beautiful. Elected silence is loveliest of all. Better even than a quiet, unpeopled daybreak, populated only by birdsong. But the silence of a locked room is inhuman.

Nell comes bringing quietly-spoken words of comfort to lift such silence. She comes bearing food and drink, fresh straw. Once in a while she brings clean linen and carries your disgusting soiled sheets away. Usually this means that someone important is on his way.

Though the girls are grateful to her, Nell knows that even the Almighty's forgiveness may be beyond her reach. In becoming wedded to Pimp, she sold her soul to the Devil. It's one story she's loth to tell. Though it'll be teased from her, soon enough.

In the meantime, Nell will serve some sort of penance. Taking her beatings without complaint. Bringing comfort to Pimp's girls. To Edie, as well.

'Helping me raise Wilburh, then Osbert and Sunny offered her the chance of redemption,' Grandmother Edie says.

But we're cantering ahead of ourselves again. Sunny has more stories to tell. The family history that he's gathered, the way we pick blackberries in autumn. He's hoarded them for the cold winter nights. A storyweaver's tales must be as multi-coloured and various as the October trees or as the feathers of a popinjay, as bright as his jongleur's patchwork coat. He has to draw breath, appraise his listeners and give them the sort of stories they long for. Whether seigneur or serf.

'I listen to what the whistle says,' he tells me. 'I let it play whichever melody it chooses. It tells my fingers where they should dance. It instructs my lips which words they should form.'

Tonight, for example, his audience will be Exeter's newly-formed guilds of metalworkers. Not the easiest of audiences. Already riven by infighting. Those who work in base lead are despised by the silversmiths, who look up only to the goldsmiths. The goldsmiths hold all the others – even the silversmiths – in polite contempt. Sunny will need to conjure a story to satisfy them all. The solution will no doubt be to ridicule their common enemy.

But wait, he says. Everyone's enemy is surely the Normans. Yet these men all rely on the Normans for their trade: especially those who forge precious metals. So he must curb his instincts and tell only a gently mocking tale.

He's forging an idea as lovingly and carefully as a man hammers a wedding ring. He'll tell the story of the Norman overlord, his lady and a group of metalworkers.

The Norman overlord opts to disappear off on a crusade, in order to earn his rightful place in paradise. But there's a problem. His wife is the loveliest, the most longed-for woman in a city of pretty women. How will he save his honour and hers while he's away? Whom can he trust? No one. So he has her locked in a chastity belt. The body of the belt will be made of tin to minimise her discomfort, the belt an impenetrable band of bronze, the rivets iron, the decorations finely worked copper, the locks dressed in silver, as befits a lady and the whole plated in gold. The belt will be graced with six locks and keys. The six different keys will be guarded by the six different metalsmiths.

Satisfied, he leaves his wife behind, but he's not reckoned on the fact that the six members of the metalworkers' guilds will work together with a bond as tough as tin, as resolute as iron, as strong as bronze, as durable as copper, as safe as silver and as precious as gold. Nor has he reckoned on her Ladyship's ingenuity (for it's only a fool who underestimates a woman).

Her Ladyship summons the six metalworkers to her chamber. In the time it takes to nail a horse's shoe to a hoof, they've thrashed out an agreement.

They'll unlock her belt (for what man in his right mind wants to see a lady suffer so?). In return, on Mondays she'll save her love for the tinsmith, on Tuesdays she'll save her love for the bronze-worker . . .

'You get the picture,' Sunny says.

On Sundays – her day of rest – she'll devote herself to the Almighty.

So the first moral of the tale is that while some spend their time in a faraway land, buying their place in paradise, others will find a piece of heaven on earth right here and now.

And the second moral of the tale is that guildsmen should work together, never be riven by infighting. Therein lies the key to betterment.

XVIII

Osbert claims he's no time for history. Never has had. Right from the moment when – unlike his sister, Wilburh - he couldn't wait to vacate his mother's womb. Not lulled by its rhythmic drumbeat. Nor soothed by its chorus of gurglings. Osbert was impatient to get on with life, to better himself.

But wait. The whistle and Sunny whisper a different tale. The whistle speaks to Sunny of history reinvented, truths being distorted.

The whistle quietly speaks to Sunny of a foundling.

Nell was there, patting Edie's perspiring brow, once more. That much is true.

She was now practised in the art of dabbing a wetted cloth on a forehead to ease the passage of childbirth.

This is called *becoming a dab hand*.

Where Wilburh smiled an unconditional smile that spoke of her being at ease with the world, Ossie peered at Nell's form with a look of curiosity or suspicion. True.

I mistrust the world and everyone in it, his gaze said.

'Yes, indeed,' Grandmother Edie confirms it. 'Ozzie was always grizzling, having taken umbrage with the world.'

But these tell only part of the story. Because the child who emerged from Edie's womb didn't look up, didn't grizzle, but emerged stillborn.

And while Edie sobbed, Nell quietly went about tidying up the mess, and then performing a miracle. She carried the child's corpse from the room. When she returned, she was carrying Ossie in her arms. No questions must ever be asked. The identity of the real mother will never, never be revealed. Edie is Ossie's mother from here on in. She'll love him not a jot less than she'll love the two children – Wilburh, and, later, Sunny – whom she bore.

The child peered first at Nell, then at his new mother and, later, at his new father, with a look of mild disapproval for having visited life upon him. Then he looked around the room and, continuing to grizzle, he let his dissatisfaction with his surroundings be known. This was understandable. A hovel's a miserable place to live in. Not much light and lots of damp. Even if love abounds there, it doesn't redeem the place.

Yes. The baby Osbert and his family were imprisoned in the room, along with the dampness seeping from the walls and the acrid smoke from the fire, as it lost its tussle with the cold and wet. Only a little of the damp and smoke managed to make its break for freedom, either through the shutter, propped open with a stick on clement days or through the cracks in the mud, daubed onto the walls. And in place of the twin ills of damp and cold come only a smattering of light and fresh air.

Osbert seemed to have his eyes forever on the four dank corners of the room, though none of the others was sure what he was searching for. Maybe, he feared the presence of boggarts or other malign spirits. Or perhaps the foundling child, because he had no beginning, was forever seeking the happy ending that would elude him. And because he began as nothing – stillborn – but, by the miracle of Nell's intervention, became a living son, he'd grow to believe that betterment was the only option open to him.

Osbert didn't yet know this, but his worst nightmare would not be one of the boggarts or pucks (which some call pucksies or pixies) waiting in the dark to ply their mischief. No, this would emerge from his new mother's womb. Sunny, would, in a little more than two years, make his entrance into the world and quickly see it as his duty to turn Osbert's look of mild disapproval into something more intense. Once he'd mastered his whistle, the one he'd be gifted by his father, Sunny would irritate the young Osbert with his shrill pipings and his mocking trills. Then, when Sunny had begun to master the art of storytelling, he'd conjure fearful tales that robbed Osbert of his sleep.

Sunny – whose disposition would match his name – would toss tales into the air as if he were a sower, scattering seed onto a ploughed field. His favourites, as night set in, would be those intended to torment Osbert, as the two of them lay side by side in their dark hovel, just at the moment Osbert (whom sleep would evade at the best of times) was thinking he might nod off. Then, having done his worst, Sunny would close his eyes, fall instantly into a snoring slumber. Not a care in the world.

'The Almighty made some men to be warriors, but he made Osbert to be his chief *worrier*,' Sunny announces. There's some truth in this. Certainly, as Overseer of the Works, Osbert's role, in adult life, will be to do the Seigneur's and the Shrike's worrying for them. Worrying materials to arrive in correct quantities. Worrying buildings to be erected on time. Worrying the coffers to be overflowing.

In the meantime, as a young Sunny span his blood-curdling, boggart-beckoning tales in order to torment his brother, Ossie, that worrying had yet to find a focus.

Osbert would, as he grew, have one thought foremost in his mind as he lay on his straw bed. And this was: to get out of their squalid little hell-hole, peopled by darkness and dampness and Sunny's wild imaginings, a place bereft of the one thing he cherished most. Apartness.

Osbert's wish would come true in time.

He'd have his own room, which he'd constantly be reminding his feckless younger brother, is made of thick, smoothly-finished and finely-decorated stone, sheltered in the curtain of the castle walls. And no number of little jibes on Sunny's part will alter this inescapable fact.

Not when Sunny mocks its proximity to the Shrike's quarters. *Within summoning distance* or *a short, fawning crawl from your lord and master.* Not even when Sunny calls it the *oublier.* The oublier being the hole cut into the basement of some Norman castles, where the vilest of offenders can be shut away and forgotten about, lobbed the occasional crust to keep them alive, simply in order to prolong their misery.

Sunny's description is unfair. And even though there's no malice in his taunts, his parents are occasionally moved to intervene.

'Enough, Sunny,' Grandmother Edie says.

'Pipe down,' Grandfather Aart says, motioning for Sunny to slip his whistle back into his belt.

It's a wonder that Uncle Osbert keeps coming back for more. A glutton, Sunny insists. Always ravenously hungry and ready to devour his mother's cooking. Forever a glutton for punishment, too.

Uncle Osbert doesn't look much like a glutton to me. As skinny as a heron, he is. Nor is his chamber anything like the *oublier* my father claims. Not that Sunny ever allows the truth to mar a tale. According to my father, the tale should wag the dogged truth.

XIX

This morning, I awoke early. Uncle Osbert rarely sleeps for long. Perhaps his restlessness has spread like a contagion as I grapple with his proposal that we be wed. As I left home, I resolved to spare him any further torment and decline his offer. Yet, how would I find the words? I've no wish to wound him.

It was only a short walk. The sun was about to rise, the mist still hovering over the meadows beyond the city walls. When most people were still rising from their beds, I could stroll along the streets, not barge and jostle my way through them. Osbert's chamber's beyond a pair of huge oak doors. They were still shut, but the keeper knows me well and allowed me passage through the small doorway.

He winked at me as I climbed through. And there, curled on the floor, Dog was sleeping. He's in love with Osbert. He forgives him all his oddities: none of which Osbert asked to be burdened with. Dog knows that Uncle Osbert's a good man. He might aim the occasional half-hearted kick Dog's way. But I swear he'd never forgive any man who hurt Dog.

Curs see what we mere humans can't. They hear voices where we hear silence. They pick up scents where we don't: whether the smell of a fox or the stench of mendacity. They see trouble brewing where we don't: the impending storm or the approaching earthquake. But most of all, curs see where love and unconditional friendship are needed most.

I knelt down beside Dog, stroked his head, and he lay back sleepily, slapping his tail against the flagstones. All a dog needs is love and food. To be allowed to love someone. To have enough food to stay his hunger pangs.

I couldn't do this to Uncle Osbert. I couldn't hurt him.

But then another voice spoke to me. A silent voice that even Dog, with his ears pricked, won't have heard. It's a memory of something Sunny said.

Osbert's chamber serves him well, Sunny observed. The cold room, cut off from the rest of the world by thick walls through which even sound struggles to pass. His room offers the rigidity, the certainty that only four stone walls can. Osbert's in love neither with people nor with any particular person, but with certainty and rigidity.

Then there's the fact that Osbert's room, shaded, north-facing, looking onto the shadowy courtyard, allows in little light.

Where Truth is the slave of Belief, there's darkness. Where Belief is the slave of Truth, there's light. There are those, such as Uncle Osbert who'll say: I believe this and that and the other. Then they'll glean only the facts that they want to hear and they crush them, squeeze them and distort them until they fit their beliefs.

Wrong, says the whistle. Wrong, says Sunny. You must take the bare-faced facts as you find them and from those facts you must fashion your beliefs.

'A mason can't carve an image in sand, Osbert,' Sunny says.

'I am Overseer of the Works,' Osbert says, dismissively. 'You're a mere storyteller, Sunny. Since when has a storyteller been able to distinguish fact from fiction?'

Now here I am, cuddling Dog, both of us seated at the door of Uncle Osbert's chamber and I've suddenly grown cold once more on the idea of being wed.

I recall, smiling to myself, how desperate Dog used to be to join our lessons. Perhaps keen to hear the voice of the man whom he craved as a master and best friend, but who seemed determined to fight the need to be loved.

'The cur has gained ingress again,' Osbert had railed. 'Perty. You are able to exercise dominion over the beast. Banish him forthwith.'

The room was still in semi-darkness, as Uncle Osbert had tripped and struck his head.

'I blame that blasted cur,' he'd snapped.

'That's not fair,' I'd protested. 'How is it his fault, Uncle Osbert?'

'It's a cur's lot to be blamed, Perty. God gave us dominion over curs so that we might blame them for our ills.'

'But you've not got dominion over the cur, Uncle Osbert,' Robin had pointed out.

'Silence, Robin,' Osbert had chastised him. 'A more pressing issue is that you have no dominion over the letters of the alphabet. Now, fetch me a candle.'

Robin had taken one from the candle box.

'Tell me, Robin. How do we spell the word *candle*?'

'I don't know how to spell one, but I know how to light it, which seems much more useful to me,' Robin had replied.

Uncle Osbert had held his head as Robin had struck the flint repeatedly over a small pile of rushes. Finally a spark had caught. Robin had held the lit rush to the candle. Then Osbert had looked up at us.

'Candles,' he'd said distractedly. 'They're here to light our path and direct us. Who directs us in our daily lives, Robin?'

'The Normans.'

'No, Robin. The Almighty.'

'Well as far as I'm concerned, the Seigneur's firstborn's more likely to strike me down for disobeying his rules than the Almighty is.'

The sound of a hunting horn had echoed in the air, sending Dog into paroxysms of wild excitement.

'It's not right to go chasing after a little fox until he's all breathless and cornered,' I'd said.

'Nonsense, Perty. The Almighty gave man dominion over the foxes.'

'Well it seems unfair to me. What would you think if I went chasing you around the room 'til you were breathless and I pinned you in the corner, Uncle Osbert?'

A strange look had come over Uncle Osbert. He'd looked as if he were about to keel over, on account of the blow to his head.

That evening, we'd eaten rock cakes, which was a rare treat. Sunny had been talking without ceasing, which was a common occurrence.

'Warm rock cakes,' Aunt Wilburh had announced. 'In my experience, a good mouthful of rock cake is one of the best ways to shut Sunny up.'

On this occasion, her recipe had failed. The rock cakes were delicious, but Sunny wouldn't stop spinning his yarns.

'Rock cakes,' he proclaimed. 'Is it not reassuring that, in these times of change – when our conquerors trample on all our best traditions and crush our faint hopes – the recipe for a rock cake is unchanged from that which our forebears used? Flour and butter worked until they become as one. Then perhaps the dregs, the slurry of Talbot's ale to give the mixture some life and levity. Let it stand. Then add honey and fruit to sweeten, eggs to bind and milk to moisten. Then warm until they're golden and that smell assails your senses. There's poetry in a rock cake.'

'Take note, children,' Aunt Wilburh said to us. 'He knows the recipe for a rock cake but not once in his whole life has he ever got off his fat little arse to bake one.'

'What my beloved sister fails to understand, children, is that a recipe doesn't make a cake. A cook does. I'm a storyteller, whereas Wilburh, besides being a thorn in my flesh, is a cook, a mother and an aunt of passing competence. As a storyteller, I piece together facts, lies, half-truths, flights of fancy and depths of thought. I stir them up, I add spice to them, I prove them, I bake them until they're ready to be devoured. It's not the facts, but the storyteller who summons the tale. The cook and not the recipe that bakes the cake.'

So. Between mouthfuls of his sister's rock cake, he regales us with the story of King Alfred and the cakes. The year was Eight Hundred and Seventy-Seven. England was at its lowest ebb.

'Remember, children. At this point in history, the Almighty had not yet invented the Normans. Oh, no. The best he could come up with then was the Vikings. As meek as newborn fawns, they were, by comparison. Yes, they raped and pillaged well enough. But the Almighty learned the error of his ways. If you're going to visit ill fortune on a nation, you need someone with the staying power of the Normans to see the job through.'

'Hang on a minute,' Talbot interrupted Sunny. 'I thought the Normans *were* Vikings, Norsemen who'd settled down in their own Dukedom across the channel.'

'Please stop clogging up my story with factual information, brother-in-law: it slows the flow,' Sunny responded, wafting his hand airily.

Alfred, King of all England was cowering on the Isle of Athelney, surrounded on all sides by salt marshes. Weakened and demoralised, he was fed on a diet of rock cakes. Left to tend to the latest batch by his hosts – a shepherd and shepherdess – he became so preoccupied with how he might transform England's ebb into something more of a flow, that he forgot the cakes, allowing them to burn. Furious with him, the shepherdess banished him from her home. Inspired by her example, he strode out and, rallying his men to the cause, sustained by his recent diet of rock cakes, he marched to Edington with a new sense of purpose. Here he routed the Danish leader, Guthrum, and his followers.

'Now here's the thing,' Sunny concluded, inspecting his own, half-eaten rock cake. 'If Wilburh had been around back then, they could have stoned the Danes with a batch of her rock cakes. That would have sent them scarpering back to Denmark.'

Uncle Osbert had, at this point, walked through the door, an angry swelling still visible on his forehead.

'Has life administered another blow to my beloved brother?' Sunny asked.

Osbert scowled in the way he continues to scowl each time Sunny lobs in one of his asides.

As the morning mist continued to clear, I turned away from Osbert's door. His proposal required more thought, before I went stumbling in. Dog shaped to follow me as I walked across the yard to begin my chores. Then he had second thoughts, as he sat down again, not wanting to be distracted from the task of teaching Uncle Osbert how to love.

XX

But back to the dim-and-distance, to a past that's been summoned (with all its flaws, its mix of fact and fable) by Sunny and his whistle.

There are good years and bad. Every once in a while, the family's stories pucker into indisputable facts. Such as the assertion that, though Sunny was too young to recall it, the year One Thousand and Ninety-Seven was a beast of a time in so many ways. The foul weather, the failure of the crops, the disease and death (among the livestock *and* the population) had all been hard to bear.

Rain and water. Too little rain and the crops will shrivel. Too much and they'll rot. Grandfather Aart says we must trust the Almighty to provide for us. Which suggests that the Almighty's attention must have been elsewhere that year, because the rain never relented. Perhaps He forgot to send the winds that move it on. And yet, water's the bringer of life.

'Thank the Almighty,' Grandfather Aart, says. 'For we had fish aplenty. Eels from the river beds, all manner of fish from the sea. The fish kept us alive that year. The fishmongers had their moment in the sun – though not literally so – while the meatmongers, the butchers, looked on in envy. I should add that the fishmongers' joy was short-lived for where there's profit, there's tax and taxes rained upon them as surely as the waters rained on them from the heavens.'

Sunny takes up the mantle. His whistle captures the sound

of the endless rain, of the few remaining cattle huddled together and lowing mournfully in the fields.

'At such times, it's cruel to be kine,' he jests.

Sunny and the whistle recount how the people without money or possessions hunkered down and tried not to think of their hunger, though their bellies were crying out angrily to their hands and mouths for not feeding them. They recall how the poorest among the population watched and waited until the fish on the stalls had begun to turn and they could barter for it or – if they happened to be in the right place at the right time – be tossed it by a fishmonger, bloated on his success.

Aart had walked alongside the Shrike, who'd sat astride his horse. The Shrike was assessing the worth of the burghers of Exeter, the men who fell within his father's demesne. He watched their transactions with his eagle's eyes. It's been said that transactions create wealth. That, without transactions, no wealth can be created. The important thing for the Shrike was to ensure he knew who became wealthy. Preferably, this should be neither the buyer nor the seller, but *him*. The lord and master.

'The man who came up with the idea of taxation should be lauded above all others, Aart,' he said.

'Apart from by those who pay tax, maistre. I imagine they're disinclined to laud him.'

'Fortunately their opinion is of no worth, Aart.'

'And if it were, then it would be taxed.'

'Count yourself blessed that I'm fond of you and I regard you more as a brother than a serf, Aart. Otherwise such insolence would not go unpunished.'

To the matter in hand. The way of establishing the correct level of taxation is straightforward. You need no grounding in arithmetic. If what's left in a common man's leather pouch, his *skrip*, needs only a cursory glance to establish its value, then that man is of no interest. If a man needs to count his coins, then he is in possession of too many and he must be disburdened by the tax system. Simple. And effectively a means of ensuring the English scum know their place. Let them learn the art of creating wealth. But let them create it for *you*, their overlord, before they gain ideas above their station.

In this, the year of incessant rains and the monotonous taste of fish, when every person and every place was possessed of a piscine stench, even the Shrike sometimes shook his head in disbelief that there should be so much suffering. Began to talk as often as any Englishman about the weather.

'By God,' he ranted, 'this constant drumming of the rain is turning my head, Aart.'

The Shrike's magnificent horse reared, as a foul, fishy beggar lurched towards them. The Shrike swung his sword angrily and struck the man's side. The beggar sank to the ground, lay still.

'Up,' the Shrike barked, demonstrating his mastery of the English tongue. He rolled his eyes as the beggar ignored him.

'Help him,' he yelled at another man, as the rain pelted down on them. The passer by pressed his fingers hard against the beggar's scrawny neck. He felt no pulse.

'Dead. Mort,' he said.

'Then take him away.'

The Shrike turned to Aart.

'Give the man a penny.'

Aart retrieved one from the skrip attached to his belt.

'God bless you,' he said to the passer-by.

The Shrike looked up into the middle distance.

'You,' he shouted, summoning over a monk.

The monk crossed himself as he beheld the dead man.

'A prayer for this wretch's soul. I've no wish that he should return to trouble my dreams . . . Another penny, Aart.' Then he turned again to the monk. 'You might also pray, for all our sakes, that my father never hears that I gave away two of his pennies. Otherwise, we'll be damned, every one of us and we may well wish we'd been as fortunate as that wretch.'

He pointed his sword towards the beggar, now draped over the passer-by's shoulder.

'To the fishmongers, Aart,' the Shrike announced. 'There are fish to be eaten and taxes to be extracted.'

XXI

'Those were indeed pitiless times,' Grandfather Aart sighs.

Pity, Sunny muses. It's perhaps what separates us from the lower order of beasts. Don't many animals feel love? A mother – any mother: take a roosting bird for example – would lay down her life for her young. But if her young are snatched from her, she knows this is the order of things. She sheds no tears. We kill to live. Life feeds on death. There's no room for mercy or pity. It's the capacity for pity, not love, that sets mankind apart from the beasts.

Yes, the year One Thousand and Ninety-Seven was a year in which pity was tested to its limits. When, according to Grandfather Aart, love was what sustained them. And perhaps the glut of fish, too.

Sunny was four then. Too young to recall the constant drumbeat of the rain that the whistle remembers with pitch perfect accuracy. Three years passed. Sunny was seven years old in the year Eleven Hundred, when, on the morning after Lammas Day, William Rufus, King of England, son of William the Conqueror died.

Two fingers, the whistle informed everyone.

Not the little finger, the wishing finger that you wrap around a chicken bone picked clean of its meat. This finger brings good luck.

Nor the third, or ring finger. This is the finger that runs to the head. It's the healing finger that must be used to stir and to apply remedies.

The second finger, the middle digit, is the one that brings ill-fortune on another. It's the finger you raise to insult an enemy.

The first finger is the poisonous or evil finger, the pointing finger that betrays another.

You must cross the first and second fingers to keep bad luck and unknown enemies at bay. But they are the two fingers that must be used to kill a man.

When you make an enemy of everyone in your realm, you should watch your back. But whose fingers will hold the arrow lightly, affix it to the bow, then draw and release it on its fateful, fatal trajectory? And who had dreamed up the plot? Was it Henry, ninth-born child and fourth-born son of the Conqueror (though the first of these facts is of interest only and no great importance because women, though they might be brighter, smarter, more feckful than men, are not deemed fit to ascend the throne)? Was it good fortune that placed Henry in the New Forest at the same time as his elder brother, William Rufus? Was it mere chance that the throne was vacated while Robert, Duke of Normandy was in Sicily and on his way home from crusading? Was it good fortune that William Rufus should keel over, there and then, allowing time for Henry to advance with unholy haste on the capital, to claim the crown?

The whistle is coy. To accuse a king is to commit treason. A man is likely to lose his head for such a claim. A whistle? It would lose its voice. Snapped in two. The whistle who wishes to retain its melody is the whistle who remains non-committal on the subject.

The church is clear on the matter. William Rufus was a godless man. It was the Almighty's will that he should die, for the Almighty's a vengeful God. You turn your back on him at your peril.

The church is a powerful foe. Too powerful. Which is why William Rufus might have striven to bring the church to its knees, stripped it of all claims to temporal jurisdiction, had he survived for long enough. Which is perhaps why he had to die . . .

Others say that Walter Tyrell shot the arrow. Here, the whistle whispers the words *scapegoat* and *covering of tracks* to Sunny.

King William Rufus was shot in the back by an arrow in the New Forest on the morning of the Second of August. That much is fact. It had proved a bad year for Rufus, but History will have to judge whether it was a bad year for everyone else. Most of the population shrugged their shoulders and couldn't care less who the ruler was. Only those with vested interests or possessions would need to fret for a while over whether their fortunes would take a turn for the better or the worse.

XXII

At the time of William Rufus's murder, when Sunny was seven years old and not yet fully master of the pipe, he was as slight as one of the pucksies he spoke of, when trying to sew the seed of fear and sleeplessness in his elder brother, Osbert's head. He was as full of devilment and trickery as one of them, too. He sneaked off invisibly to places no one else went. Wherever his whistle led him. He tiptoed through corridors, unseen, slipped through secret passageways, settled down and began to play. He gave comfort to the comfortless, met the needs of the needy, soothed the troubled souls of those seeking solace, gifted company to the lonely and unloved. And in return, all he asked for was a story.

He knew he must give the poor souls he found in those dark rooms – Pimp's girls – the freedom they craved. These girls with whom he shared a home. It would take time to liberate them. A city can't be built in moments. It must be planned, stone by stone and timber beam by timber beam.

The saddest stories sometimes lurk in the darkest of places. Sunny had thought he'd explored every nook and every cranny over the years. Ten years had passed since he'd first been handed the whistle, seven years had passed since the death of William Rufus. Sunny and his whistle had searched not just the house but the blind alleys and dank spots where hopelessness and forlornness were hidden from Respectability's contemptuous gaze. He'd unearthed tales of orphaned girls, of trust misplaced, of advantage taken and chains secured. Girls who'd held on to the hand that reached out to them in their moment of greatest need. A hand that they'd hoped would haul them to safety, but which had led them down a dark corridor and then slapped their faces when they'd protested. Lips that had promised comfort, seduced them into believing life would look up, but life had looked down on them and poured scorn on them. They'd been used. Then abuse of the verbal kind had rained on them: they were told they were sluts and whores and they'd no idea why that should be.

In the deepest recesses lay a secret that even the whistle was unable to uncover until many years of probing.

Wan and Tway.

They were housed right at the back of the rambling house, in a room more or less bereft of natural light, with its high walls reaching all the way to the cross-beam. Pimp's very own *oublier*. Their skin was as pale as the petals of wood sorrel. Their eyes spoke of a loveless life. They held on to one another, as Sunny – who'd shimmied up into the roof space, danced across the beams – lowered himself by a rope into their room. They'd heard the creaking of the beams as he's scampered across them as deftly as a rodent, then a pause as he'd secured the rope and descended, and then the gentle thud as his feet had touched the earth floor. They'd listened as he'd struck his flint repeatedly, until he'd lit a rush to light the candle he'd placed there. They'd barely breathed as he'd lifted the strange, battered tube of wood to his lips and played a tune as the candle lit up his face. Music. They weren't conscious of ever having heard it before. It was sweeter than the sound of any human voice.

Only Sunny understood what the whistle was saying. This is what it told him.

Water, wind and fire, it whispered.

It was mastery of the water and bridling of the wind that carried our forebears over the waves to England. But it was the seawater that cursed us by visiting the Normans upon us.

Water and wind bless us with life and breath. But water drowns the life from a man and wind blows his house down. And water and wind can also inflict a slow, sadistic death; weathering a rock or undermining the fabric of a house.

The whistle paused to draw breath.

Be warned, though. It's fire – not water or wind – that we should fear most. Yes, a fledgling fire can be quelled by water or wind. But a roaring fire's free to go where it chooses. The imprisonment of fire might have sparked the flame of civilisation. But fire can't be enslaved for ever. Fire's an angry, resentful prisoner. Fire will have its revenge. It will swallow you. Devour you.

Sunny put down the whistle because, having said its piece, it was now demanding a story. Two stories. There must be ghosts in the room. He held the candle in front of himself. Searched the first three corners and then waited a moment, summoned the courage to hold it towards the fourth.

He swallowed a scream before it could form, dropped the candle and, in so doing, set alight the rushes on the earth floor. Began stamping like a dervish until he'd snuffed the flames.

What he didn't yet know is that the whistle, who so prided itself on being able to tease a story from the most unlikely of places, had met its match. As he lit the candle again, he told them they shouldn't fear him.

He'd looked at both girls. And though it was hard to tell them apart – both pale, tiny and haunted by the absence of light or a life worthy of the name – he'd felt an irresistible pull the moment he'd looked in the face of the one on the left.

Sunny says it's called *love at first sight*. Osbert, curling his lip, says it's called *a sex-starved homunculus pinning his hopes on the first girl who doesn't rebuff his advances.*

'Why Wan and not Tway then?' Sunny demands to know.

'I suspect Tway cast you a withering glance and even you and that stupid whistle had enough sense to see she wasn't interested,' Osbert says.

The whistle had tried to coax the stories of their lives from Wan and Tway, but they wouldn't speak. Sunny's heard it told that some pasts, some secrets are so awful that they must be placed securely under lock and key. His whistle can only open unlocked doors. Not doors that are locked, bolted, barred and nailed.

The first time he descended into Wan's and Tway's room, Sunny brought music and light (albeit the modest light thrown by a flickering candle). He claims that, by way of reward for his efforts, he unearthed *love at first sight*, too, but that's a matter of opinion.

The second time, he at least thought to bring food.

This city's blessed with its fair share of mongers, foremost among them the gossipmongers, scandalmongers and scaremongers. There's not much profit to be gleaned from these trades. Generally, one can only barter gossip for gossip, though pennies have been known to pass hands for a rather plump, ripe and juicy portion of the fruitiest tittle-tattle. There's more money to be had mongering meat and fish, for example. Enough profit, if you're a successful meat vendor, to render it no more than a minor irritation if a passing waif filches a cooked capon while you're distracted by the hubbub behind you.

Was it a sin to steal a capon? To watch Wan's and Tway's bemusement melt into delight as the lovely fragrance greeted them? Was it wrong to have stayed their hunger pangs and to have conjured vague memories of something they'd once eaten as children? No.

Some sins are bad. Some sins are good.

Sunny will feed them up. Just like his mother, Edie, he believes in causes. His mission will be to restore these two lost souls. In return, he hopes that they'll reward him with their stories. If not stories, then their gratitude – and maybe in Wan's case, her love – will be more than enough reward.

XXIII

Perhaps imagination's a commodity not easy to come by. Perhaps you have to mine for it, the way they mine, in the West Country hills hereabouts, for the tin and lead and suchlike that brings traders from foreign climes.

Pimp's shepherd and shepherdess father and mother had named their sons according to their numerical sequence. And Pimp – in the language of shepherds – was number five.

So it was with the two girls who came into his possession. One and Two. Wan and Tway. When they were stood in front of him, perhaps four and five years old, two newly-orphaned girls, two complete strangers who shared only a common history of misfortune, Pimp had looked into their eyes and been moved. Just as Sunny would be, in the future. But whereas Sunny had imagined love at first sight, Pimp had seen, deep in their brown eyes, shadowed by poverty and hunger, something called *profit at first sight*.

Pimp had had them locked away. In an otherwise merciless act, he'd at least confined the two strangers to one room, so that they had the blessing of company.

As meat must be left in a dark, cool place, slowly to tenderise until it reaches it's full, soft, savoury, tumble-over-the-tongue maturity and it's ready to be devoured, so these two must be placed into storage and nurtured until they've reached their flavoursome best and a customer – Pimp has the particular customer in mind – is ready to pay a veritable fortune to impale them.

They must be slim, their flesh must be as pale as moonlight and – yes, wealthy Norman clients will demand this – their skin must bruise to a lovely blue-black. It's imperative that they've learned (just as a hound must learn) to take their beatings without complaint and continue to look lovingly and gratefully into your eyes, whatever befalls them.

Then, when the man who abused you has paid Pimp his dues and is ready to leave, you must accept that the guilt is all yours. Not his. You are an irredeemable sinner and a whore, now. The customer was a man with needs. This is the order of things.

Nell had never heard of Moses or Mount Sinai or the Ten Commandments. She knew, without having to be told, what's right and wrong. Right is that which makes the lives of others just a little brighter, that which makes them feel a mite more loved. Wrong is that which, in diminishing others, diminishes you.

It ate away at her. Those two girls. Two strangers, united now by fear as well as a common history of misfortune. Both imprisoned. Nell was the one who held the key. But fear stopped her from ushering them to their freedom. Fear of incurring Pimp's wrath. Although her sin of cowardice is only a small sin (because there are sins as small as ripples and sins as huge as tidal waves), it is nevertheless a sin.

Nell sought redemption by helping Edie and her three children, by not intervening, years later, when she suspected the youngest of the three – the pucksy who played his pipe – of offering comfort and food to Wan and Tway and the other girls. She might have sought Redemption, but Redemption looked down on her with disgust and spurned her advances. Edie, on the other hand, remained grateful for Nell's help. Regarded her as a friend.

'I'm beyond forgiveness,' Nell whispered, as she sat down beside Edie, wringing her hands.

'There's a saying, Nell. To know all is to forgive all.'

This isn't strictly true, of course. The Almighty's omniscient and yet he condemns many of us to hell.

'Tell me, Nell.'

Nell shaped to speak. At first sobs emerged. Sobs that had been waiting for years to see the light of day. Slowly, they gave way to words.

The first thing that ever happened to Nell was being immersed into a pale of water until she'd ceased breathing. Had the water been as warm as a womb, then this might have been an almost pleasant experience. The water had, in fact, been cold. The shock had stopped her heart in its tracks.

'I lost my heart, Edie. I became heartless.'

She lost her mother, too. She'd already lost her father within moments of being conceived when he'd pulled up his leggings, tossed Nell's young mother a penny and grunted.

Nell's second experience on entering this life was to be thrown onto a midden, where she'd lain, left for dead, drying in the sun. Drowned and thrown onto the rubbish heap the way a kitten might be.

But then the miracle of her resurrection had occurred.

It must have been the warmth of the sun. Perhaps it was destiny. Perhaps it was just bad luck that she should have survived.

'Pimp found me. Pimp is my Redeemer,' she said.

He was passing. Pimp always searched in the most unseemly places to find his girls. Hopelessness is a happy, hopeful hunting ground for a Pimp.

He saw the newborn baby flinch, picked her up, held her upside down and emptied her lungs.

'And that was when I became fodder, retrieved from the midden.'

A woman of Pimp's acquaintance, whose breasts were swollen with undrunk milk, would be given pennies for feeding Nell. There was one condition. The wet nurse must guard against falling in love with her baby, because they'd be separated soon enough.

So Nell was fed only with the milk of human unkindness. The other variety was denied her.

Already heartless, she was now loveless.

As soon as Nell was old enough to fend herself, she came into Pimp's ownership.

'This is where Pimp's plan went slightly awry,' she says. 'All the other girls despised him, because they were his slaves. They feared him, but they felt they owed him nothing. He'd taken from them: their lives, their dignity, their daylight, their hope. They'd have happily trampled over their master to grasp a better life. I was different. He was my Redeemer. He'd made me born again. I owed him my life. He knew I felt beholden to him. I thought this meant I might be allowed to love him and that he might love me in return. Instead it meant I was his to do with as he pleased.'

'But he didn't, did he?' Edie asked. 'I thought he'd spared you the fate of the other girls.'

'My fate was worse. I'm not talking about the bullying and the beatings he feels he can give me and I must take, because I owe him my life . . .'

'What then?'

'I'm his stale.'

A stale, as foul a thing as curdling milk.

Edie had no idea what a stale might be.

'A lure, in human form, Edie.'

Pimp could summon anger readily enough and he could engender fear with a single blow to the body. But he couldn't conjure trust.

Guile was needed when ensnaring the new girls. Nell was required. She was the bait, or stale, who reeled the girls in.

'I lured them in here, Edie. I'm the one who bears Pimp's sins.'

This isn't how it's supposed to be. The Redeemer is supposed to bear the sins of the redeemed. And not the reverse.

'I'm the very devil. It's no wonder the girls despise me. I despise myself.'

'I know a man of God who'll gladly offer you absolution,' Edie said.

'And what of the girls?'

'They need no forgiveness. Only their freedom.'

Though Edie was unsure how they might gain that.

In the meantime, she'd perhaps try to show Nell how to be loved. Just as, more than thirty years later, Dog will patiently be trying to teach Osbert – older but no wiser in matters of the heart – how to allow himself to be loved.

XXIV

There's a reason they call a *deadline* by that name.

You're given choices. Your life can go off in one trajectory or another. But once the arrow's been shot, its course is set, for better or for worse. Some talk of crossroads, of branches forking from the highway, which suggests that you can retrace your steps and try again. This is called *learning from the error of your ways*. Whether those are highways or byways.

Uncle Osbert was a stickler for accuracy. Take your time. Make the right decision. No going back. This was a deadline because I was being offered the choice between one of two lives. If I embraced one life, then I'd be sentencing my other life to death.

One of my life lines would be dead.

The life of sterile certainties, cold comforts and a loveless marriage. Or another life in which – if Grandmother Edie's abbess was right – the swell of joy and the dip of sadness, the lift of love and the hurt of hardship – are balanced in some sort of harmony.

The life of a butterfly, buffeted by breeze and bluster, ruined by rain but sometimes brightened by blazing sun and blue sky. Or the certainty and measured predictability of life corralled in a cramped cocoon. Wasn't this the choice my grandmother and grandfather were faced with when they took flight from their cloistered existence?

Osbert had summoned Sunny and me to his chamber. As Overseer of the Works, he'd become adept at summoning folks. Osbert basked in the glow of the Shrike's anger with those who failed to do his clerk's bidding.

'Allow me to be direct,' Osbert began. 'Five days have elapsed. It's time for Perty to confirm whether or not she wishes to accept my offer that she should be elevated above her mean station and become wife to an Overseer of the Works.'

'What say you, Perty?' Sunny responded.

'I'm flattered that Uncle Osbert should have condescended to offer his hand to one as mean and lowly as I am. I'm touched by his thoughtfulness in offering me five days in which to ponder a life with him. I'm grateful to Uncle Osbert for teaching me to read and write and for giving me a smattering of Latin and French, but I couldn't consent to be wed to a man who doesn't think to accept me for what I am, rather than what I might be. Not once has Uncle Osbert spoken of love.'

'Well said, Perty,' Sunny agreed. 'Ossie proposed with his head. Not his heart.'

'If I might be so bold,' Uncle Osbert persisted, 'a marriage should be based on practical considerations, not on passing fancies or passions. Perty is showing a measure both of ill judgement and ingratitude.'

'Bollocks,' Sunny said. 'What Perty's shown is good sense and a heavy dollop of spirit. Go tell your overlord he can stick his plan where the sun never shines. For God's sake, Ossie. Are you really so dense?'

A look of steely resolution came over Osbert.

'You are both dismissed,' he said. 'And don't let the cur in as you leave.'

I was trembling, as we walked home. My father placed a comforting arm around me.

'The whistle says you've had what we call *a lucky escape*,' he said. 'Don't doubt yourself, Perty. You've chosen well.'

There were awkward silences when Osbert graced our home with his presence that night. I swear Dog looked at me wistfully. Perhaps – given that curs know a lot that we don't – he'd concluded that the three of us – Osbert, he and I – could have bumbled along happily together.

Thankfully, Talbot, blissfully unaware of the earlier exchange, prattled on blindly. Some tale about how he'd been excavating the tunnel that runs from the east gate of the city to the castle, when he'd lost his bearings and burrowed upwards when he should have been working forwards, emerging slap bang in the middle of the biggest midden you ever saw. Dusted himself down and carried happily on.

'And that,' he concluded, 'was one great heap of rubbish.'

Sunny, who'd left the floor to Talbot, picked up his whistle, placed it to his lips. To my mind, he played a tune that spoke of wedding bells unrung, proposals spurned. Love that must emanate from the heart and not the head.

It was hard answering back to the whistle when it was determined to have the last word.

Osbert scowled at his younger brother.

I looked at the ground, feeling ashamed. Perhaps even mourning my dead life line.

Dog sidled over to me and rested his head on my lap.

He could teach each and every one of us about love.

Part Two

LIPS

I

I felt mortified at having had to hurt Uncle Osbert's feelings so badly. Many would say a girl's lot is to make a man happy. Especially an essentially good and well-meaning man such as Uncle Osbert. Some would say the fault lies with my being able to read and write, for that's given me ideas above my station in life. But I believe we should all be free to choose whom we spend our wedded lives with. A butterfly encased in a dark cocoon would be the saddest sight to behold. How can a girl make a man happy when she has no joy to bring him? You can't conjure love. You can't force it to be where it doesn't wish to be. It's not something that should be tamed and subdued. Love's wilder and freer than even the wind. It goes where it wills.

'I'm sorry,' I muttered to Uncle Osbert.

When he looked at me, there was pain in his eyes. But it seemed to me it was the pain of a man humiliated, not one who mourned the loss of love. Had he looked at me with longing, I might even have relented in a moment of weakness. I might have shrugged my shoulders and thought: Osbert will provide for me and I for him. I'd perhaps have thought: so long as he loves me, then I might grow to love him, for being loved can change a person in ways they've not suspected. In the way the wild and untamed storm can bend a strong, resolute tree.

'You're still Perty's favourite uncle,' Grandmother Edie said, embracing him. 'It's just that Perty's not inclined to be wed.'

Uncle Osbert looked as if he wished to shrink from view.

Uncle Talbot then spoke up.

'Hang on a minute. Perty only has two uncles. If Ossie's the favourite, what does that make me?'

II

'Where were we, Perty?' Sunny asks.

'Nell was helping Grandmother Edie to raise her children, while Grandfather Aart was bettering himself to provide for them. Though his search for Truth seemed to be flagging a little,' I remind him.

'Ah, yes,' he says, playing a little triplet on his whistle.

Wilful Aunt Wilburh had been the firstborn, testing Aart and Edie's patience to the limit. Uncle Osbert had been next. The foundling, but no less loved, who'd filled a void left by a stillborn child. Then Sunngifu, as sunny and carefree as a warm summer's day.

There's one school of thought that says rules exist merely to beg questions. If you intend to break them, then you must offer up a sound reason as to why this should be so. If we fail to break rules, we fail to grow.

Wilburh believes in breaking rules. At every opportunity. But, having the gift of the gab, she always has her excuse at the ready.

Osbert believes that rules are there to be adhered to with a commitment as rigid as he is, as he stands there, petrified by most things: love, touch, uncertainty. If it's not there, written in black and white, then Osbert's paralysed by fear of it.

'Osbert's as hidebound as one of those buckskin tomes he pores over in the cathedral library,' Wilburh laughs.

Sunny – easy-going Sunny – watches and learns. Pipes his

whistle as he mulls over the options. Listens to the whistle's advice. Steers a middle course.

Osbert showed no interest in girls, but seemed to be in love with rules, with books (which his father had taught him to read and which the brothers in the minster had encouraged him to study) and with numbers and all their certainty. Wilburh, though, had other interests.

A young lad should pursue a maiden, shouldn't he?

Not the lads she knew. By and large they were too timorous or more interested in *things* than they were in you. More concerned, too, with their mock sword fights with the stalks of waybread, or plantain, that stubbornly grows even on the streets. In such circumstances, a girl has to take matters in hand. She mustn't be too pushy. Because if she is, the boys will call her either a *nag* or – worse still – a *hussy*. It requires a lot of craft, does reeling in a boy.

There are tried and tested methods. Such as encouraging your best friend (a girl) to tell his best friend (a boy) that you quite like him. This invariably arouses the boy's interest. And the thing about boys is that they're easily flattered and they're also generally bone idle good-for-nothings.

So, having dangled the bait and got him nibbling, you should shrug your shoulders and pretend you don't care. But you must be watchful. Your shrug must be of the *might be interested if you keep on at me* type and not the *get lost* sort. Although woefully bad at understanding the unspoken word, boys should at least be able to distinguish the two shrugs. These were the rules.

Wilburh preferred to do things her own wilful way, though. She didn't need outside help. Having lived with two brothers, she understood the looks one had to call on. Talbot was the boy for her. Moody, dark and handsome. She'd smile at him encouragingly, flatter him every now and again, but keep him guessing. The object of all this is to conjure longing. All young boys – with the notable exception of Osbert – feel longing. A boy who doesn't ache with longing most of the day and a fair chunk of the night isn't a normal boy. So the trick is to make him understand that his isn't a vague longing for girls in general or a pressing need for a rough and tumble with any girl who'll say: *yes*. He must be made to understand that his longing and your presence are as one. Persuade him slowly that he can't live a further moment without you. Don't be in a fevered rush, because most boys are slow-witted when it comes to matters of the heart.

Talbot was in animated conversation with Sunny and some other lads about every boy's preferred mode of transport, but one that's beyond the means of every peasant. In the absence of a horse, your two ill-shod feet will have to do. But that doesn't stop your dreaming of sitting astride your very own thoroughbred, seated in some soft, shiny, supple leather shoes.

Boys are unlikely to be swayed by practicality. They all dream of owning and driving a horse faster and sportier than the rest.

'I want a horse I can dig my heels into and have it galloping faster than the wind,' Talbot said.

'Mine would be faster and sleeker than yours,' Sunny bragged. 'It'd go from a standing start to the speed of lightning in moments. What about you, Ossie?'

Ossie ignored their babbling. There was no place for horses – even piebald palfreys – in Ossie's black-and-white world. No place for childish dreams.

'What about you, Wilburh?' Sunny persisted.

'Don't care,' Wilburh replied, 'so long as it's a nice colour.'

'Typical girl,' Sunny scoffed. But Wilburh hadn't finished.

'I reckon I'd like a black one with a nice sheen to it . . . I don't know. Maybe the same colour as Talbot's hair.'

Talbot stopped thinking about horses for a moment.

'Of course,' Wilburh continued, 'being a girl, I wouldn't know how to ride it properly, so I'd need to sit behind someone and hold on to him for my dear life.'

Wilburh strode off. The first twitch on the bait. She'd reel Talbot in soon enough. She turned away and – as she walked off – she heard one of the other boys muttering that he swore Wilburh had her eye on Talbot. His words were full of bravado but his voice conveyed doubt as to whether or not it was true. None of the boys had any idea. Least of all Talbot.

Uncle Osbert has no time for Sunny's stories. Reminiscing? What's the point? Whoever bettered themselves by being immersed in the past, he asks.

'The only things we should glean from the past are lessons,' he says. 'Lessons – our successes and failures – are the ingredients that fuel our betterment. Stories are for fools such as Sunny, who wallow in them the way a pig wallows in mud.'

'What about History lessons then?' Sunny asks.

'I don't think I'll be coming to you for many of those,' Osbert says, 'bereft as they are of any fact.'

'Stop it, you two,' Grandmother Edie intervenes.

Sunny begins to play a melody on his whistle. His eyes are closed. The whistle will be speaking to him of abandonment, of pasts wallowed in, of the joy to be garnered from living for the moment.

Later, Osbert made an announcement as he shaped to leave.

'I've come to the decision that there's nothing further to be gained from teaching my three charges. It seems to me a thankless undertaking for which I elicit little or no gratitude. Tomorrow's tutorial will be my last.'

'I'm grateful for everything you've done, Uncle Osbert,' I said. 'And I'm sorry.'

He shrugged his shoulders but I knew he was hurting inside.

III

I went about my morning chores with a heavy heart. My thoughts weren't on the here-and-now as I stepped, left foot first, from our home. You should always remember to step from any place with your right foot first, for to do otherwise is to risk ill fortune. I knew, already, that I would miss having the lessons with Uncle Osbert. For some of us, there's joy to be had each time we learn something fresh and new. Others, such as Robin, might be vexed by the challenge of mastering some skill or acquiring a new piece of knowledge. I devour learning as a beggar tears into scraps. Yes, for all that they could often be as dull and grey as a thunder cloud, I shall miss having my lessons with Uncle Osbert.

Normally, I love the steady rhythms of the day. The comfort of its certainties, over-layered with the pleasure of the slowly changing seasons. I rise each morning glad to have work that's a joy to undertake, but – unlike scribing or arithmetic – it fails to nourish me.

From the age of eleven, I've tended the animals that are kept within the castle bailey. I love their stench, their bleatings and their eager pleading as I come to them. I gather the eggs that must be hatched, not eaten, and place them where the broody hens will sit on them, for hens are absentminded. I feed the other animals, each to their kind, with grain or hay. I love the orphaned or rejected lambs, kids and calves most, and wean them with milk. Then I must muck out and tidy the yard.

I do this – day after day – with love in my heart. Love for the Almighty's gentle creatures and love of life, however hard that sometimes might be. Yet today I'm sad because the lessons that I so looked forward to are to be ended.

Eadwerd, Robin and I broke off from our chores to learn, for the last time, of numbers and words and their like. To Robin and probably to Ed this will have seemed a blessing. But not to me. I know that I'm a mere girl. I know that some think I might have expected already to have taken on the burden of being wed and being a mother, but Sunny has said not to be in a rush to wish my childhood away.

Like a penny dropped in the teeming city streets, a childhood lost is a childhood that'll never be found again, he says.

Uncle Osbert only mustered a half-smile as he welcomed us to his quarters.

'Are you having a strop on account of Perty turning her nose up at marrying you, Uncle Osbert?' Robin asked.

I wanted to die of shame. So did Uncle Osbert. Robin didn't even register our embarrassment. Which makes him cursed twice over: for opening his mouth when he shouldn't have and for being without a brain.

Uncle Osbert coughed and tried to compose himself.

'Enough, Robin,' he said. 'Let bygones be bygones. Today, I would warn my young charges of perils that lie in wait. Ere long the annual fair will be upon us. Those of us who are given to lives of sobriety have every reason to fear times such as these, when the devil is at his most active, recruiting new black sheep to his fold.'

'What about them that don't 'spouse sobriety but don't 'spouse the devil either?' Robin asked. 'I reckon I might be one of them.'

'Such men are deluded, Robin. Now, to the matter in hand. Demons will come to our city for the fair, peddling falsehoods, purveying all manner of evil. Temptation will be placed before you, but the pedlars and their ilk would fleece every man or woman who crosses their path. Perty. You, in particular, must guard your virtue.'

'We'll guard Perty for you, Uncle Osbert,' Robin piped up.

'I believe that Perty's more than capable of guarding her own honour, Robin. I'm merely proffering a gentle reminder. Enough of your prattling. We shall now recap on what you've learned under my tutelage. In your case, Robin, this will take rather less time than it will for your two colleagues.'

It seemed to me that I had reason to be grateful to Uncle Osbert, because Eadwerd and I could read and write with some proficiency, though the words themselves, being generally in Latin made not much sense. This, Uncle Osbert said, was not a problem, though I wasn't so sure about that. Being able to read and write but not in the tongue that you can understand is about as useful as having just one leather shoe.

'Robin has learned the letter x,' Uncle Osbert said. 'This will serve him well if ever he needs to sign a contract. Whether he reads the contract in English or Latin, its meaning will prove elusive. As for the rest of the alphabet, I doubt that this will be called upon in his work as an apprentice builder. Being an apprentice carver, Eadwerd will have more call to use the alphabet as a whole. Its meaning will, however, not need to be understood. As for Perty: although she is the most able of you and is an accomplished grammarian who writes with a tidy script, I see no earthly reason why, being a woman, she should ever now be called upon to understand a written word in any language.'

I cooled in my feelings towards Uncle Osbert again as he said that, even though I knew he was speaking the truth, rather than criticising me. Sometimes there are good and bad ways to put things. Uncle Osbert can normally be relied on to put things badly, even though he means well.

IV

Life soon returns to normal, Sunny says. Worrisome thoughts shouldn't be given house room.

'We must rejoice in our blessings,' he told me. 'Like those freckles on your cheeks, there are more blessings than you could ever count, Perty.'

'I've never had a blessing,' Robin piped up.

'What about your life and health and the love of your family, Robin?' Wilburh challenged him.

'All right then. I've had three blessings.'

'That in itself is a blessing, then,' Talbot added, 'because I doubt that Robin can count much beyond three.'

Sunny turned to me, again.

'Life's like a sack of grain, Perty. If you take a cup of grain from the sack,' he explained, 'what's left falls neatly into place. It's looks for all the world as if nothing's changed.'

Though you know it has, of course. You've taken a cup of grain, so what's left must be diminished, however things might seem.

'We must all look on the bright side,' Sunny persisted. 'Tonight, having donned my jongleur's coat, I'll summon a cheery tale. Perhaps remind everyone about Ossie and last year's annual fair.'

'That would be cruel,' I protested.

'Mockery's only cruel if it ever reaches the ears of the person being mocked. Otherwise it's just good honest mirth,' Sunny insists.

We still all recall the way Osbert shouted at the itinerants last year.

'Vipers. Charlatans. Foxes,' he ranted. Then he turned to the crowd. 'Be not deceived by their lies and trickery.'

We were so ashamed that we wanted to curl up and die. It didn't help matters that Uncle Osbert's been cursed with a reedy voice that struggles to command authority. Dog was standing beside Osbert and barking furiously at the itinerants. Everyone else was thinking: we know they're all thieves and tricksters, but we just want to have some fun.

What Uncle Osbert fails to understand is that most people would walk over hot coals to keep the fair, because the main benefit of the celebration is that no one – neither the men nor the apprentices – has to go to work for the week. The women and girls must continue to do their chores, of course, but such is the way of the world.

V

The fair was soon upon us and Uncle Osbert's worst fears would undoubtedly be realised.

'At last,' Uncle Talbot said. 'A chance for me to take it easy for five days.'

'In all the time I've known you, you've never done anything *but* take it easy,' Aunt Wilburh scoffed. Talbot's immune to her barbs. It's like nettle stings. You get enough of them and you cease to feel them after a while. Although the truth is that Uncle Talbot's never once *grasped the nettle* in his whole, lazy life.

'You must be a saint,' Aunt Wilburh continued.

'I've had my moments, but I suppose I'm what they call a *good sort*,' Uncle Talbot said. 'A saint, eh? Never quite thought of myself as that, but, if you say so, my love.'

'Yes, I do say so and I'll tell you why. They say there's no rest for the wicked. Since resting is all you do, you must be entirely free of wickedness.'

Uncle Talbot scowled, but the truth is that he enjoys Wilburh's barbs.

He winked at me. Then explained a thing or two about bickering.

You might think bickering – like arguing – calls for two participants, he says. Bullying, too. You need a bully and a victim. Even nagging isn't possible without both the nag (who, more often than not, has good grounds for complaint) and the nagged (who normally needs a good kick up his – yes, always *his* – slothful arse).

'I'm what they call *the exception to the rule*,' Talbot said proudly, inviting Eadwerd and Robin to join us. 'Look at me. Do I ever summon one word in my defence, children? No. Talbot takes his punishment without complaint. He's the missing half of a lop-sided argument. Talbot is unique in being *bicked upon*.'

Bicked upon by all and sundry, as it happened. Not just by Wilburh.

Uncle Talbot had always been odd, but in a rather different way to Uncle Osbert. Where no one (with the exception of Grandmother Edie) was ever at ease with Osbert, Uncle Talbot seemed to be regarded differently by adults and children.

'Be wary of your Uncle Talbot,' Osbert had warned us. But, then again, Osbert was wary of everyone and everything.

Sunny called Uncle Talbot *Ofertalbot*, the word *ofertael* meaning *odd number*. Odd number. Oddball. Never one to get even. The arrow of Sunny's wit with its poisoned tip didn't rile Talbot. Like those harmless nettle stings. Or like Wilburh's bickerish barbs.

Robin, Eadwerd and I had never seen any reason to be wary of Uncle Talbot. Nor did we find it odd that he sat in the gloomiest corner of the room, talking to us. Peering at us as he did so.

'I'll let you into a secret,' he'd say. 'Before I lived this miserable, bicked-upon life, what do you think I was? In my former, happier life, I was a mole.'

Yes, you could see, when he peered at you in the gloom, that this might have been true.

'I may have long, unkempt hair and a beard as rough as a badger's coat, but try stroking the hair on the back of my hands.'

We'd do as we were bidden.

'Does that not feel like a mole's pelt?'

It did, now he'd mentioned it.

'And look at my grubby nails, ingrained with dirt. What does that tell you?'

'It tells you he never washes his hands,' Aunt Wilburh would shout across at us.

'Don't listen to her. I'm being bicked upon,' Talbot would whisper. 'These used to be a mole's talons.'

'A mole must spend his whole time burrowing,' Uncle Talbot would explain. 'You children must keep burrowing your way through life. You must hope for other delights around the corner.'

He'd sigh.

'In my last life as a soft-pelted, sharp-taloned mole, oh how happily I tunnelled day after day. Oh how my snout twitched when I found a juicy earthworm. These days I hope not for earthworms but for sunlit days when I'm not bicked upon by all and sundry.'

He'd such a forlorn look to him, we'd have done anything to please him.

'Let me show you my swollen veins,' he'd say, removing the leather straps and taking off his leggings, much to the consternation of Uncle Osbert in particular.

'Trace your fingers over them,' Uncle Talbot would tell us. 'You may imagine these are like mighty rivers, meandering their way over my legs. But these are my hopes and dreams, burrowing away, getting under my skin.'

I'd shape to touch my uncle's swollen veins, with a mixture of inquisitiveness and revulsion, excitement and dread.

'In the name of the Almighty, Talbot,' Wilburh would chastise him. 'Please replace your pants.'

Nagging? Bickering? Bullying? Either way, Talbot would obey her without complaint.

VI

The annual summer fair has arrived. Osbert's charlatans have descended like a swarm of locusts. Indeed, there's a buzz about the place. A low hum of excitement.

We know we're going to have every last silver coin stripped from us. We don't care, because losing the few pennies you own is worth it. You can't buy much when you don't have much. But hope and excitement are just about affordable.

Robin, Eadwerd and I wandered among the stalls. Listening to the strange accents of the stall owners, the pedlars, the magicians, the fortune tellers. Marvelling at the unfamiliar animals – living creatures from faraway lands or unborn beasts with two heads, pickled in vinegar. Then Robin and Eadwerd went off to find the same mermaid they'd seen for each of the previous two years. She'd always appeared bored by the whole idea of sitting down and being gawked at all day. Furthermore, she'd looked to me like a girl wearing a fabric tail cut out to look like scales. And though she'd just sat there looking into a mirror, Robin seemed determined that he'd marry her one day. Why he should want to marry a mermaid, I can't be sure.

'You wouldn't understand,' he scoffed at me.

I don't suppose he'd spent one moment thinking about how his sea-dwelling wife would get about the city. There was also the possibility that no mermaid in her right mind would want to marry Robin.

'Have you considered that she might turn you down?' I pressed him.

'If she does, then I'll settle for you, Perty,' he said.

'You've more chance of landing the mermaid,' I said.

I wandered off on my own. I love the smells of food being cooked. Meats such as rarely pass my lips. Sometimes, when I was a child, a stall owner would smile and hand me a scrap of food such as only a Norman could normally hope to enjoy. Nowadays that's not so wise.

'You're a young woman, Perty,' my father, Sunny, told me. 'There are men who'll hand you scraps of meat and expect favours in return. A maiden must be beholden to no man. Therein lies the path to her ruin.'

After a while, I sat in the shade of my favourite oak tree. It stands just outside the city walls and I've rested there many a time, listening to the muffled shouts coming from within the city. It's always been my favourite tree, so large I can't even get my arms around it when I hug it. Nor can Eadwerd and he's now grown taller than me.

Eadwerd was what Sunny calls *late to blossom*. Where I shot up, he took his time. He never rushes in, does Eadwerd.

'You were ever the creature of passions and impulses, Perty,' Sunny said. 'Eadwerd bides his time until he's sure of a thing and then, once his mind's made up, there's no changing it. You're like the silver birch, all slim and supple and ladylike, and Ed is like the slower-growing oak. Silent and strong.'

Ed carved my name on my favourite tree two years ago and I can still make it out very clearly, though only because I know where to look. I watched him at work as he did it. He used his chisel and mallet. It's no wonder that Eadwerd's been taken on as an apprentice carver. His hand's so steady. He hammers with his left hand and guides the chisel with his right.

'You must promise me you'll not tell Uncle Osbert I use my sinister hand, Perty,' he'd said to me, as if he were committing a sin.

I suspect Uncle Osbert's definition of a sin is anything he doesn't do. And possibly quite a lot that he does do, as well.

'I imagine the Almighty's not fussed about your using your left hand,' I said to Eadwerd. 'Besides. I doubt he'd have made it so good at wielding a mallet if he didn't want you to use it.'

I was remembering this as I sat in the shade of my oak tree, when I found myself listening to the voice of a pedlar. Commerce spills out even beyond the city walls at the time of the fair. The pedlar was holding up some grubby old pieces of bone. Not clean like a bone that's just had the meat picked off it by a cur. This one was jaundiced by the years.

The pedlar was telling us all that these were not mere bones that he was offering us, but something much more precious. What they call *relics*.

'Friends,' he said, and his voice was like a melody, 'I sell Hope and the promise of rapturous joy in an afterlife more glorious than this miserable one. Though be warned. The afterlife of which I speak will make this life seem one of easy indolence if you, my friends, make the wrong choices and condemn yourselves to the pit of despair we call hell.'

That sounded at least worth a hard-earned penny.

He told us he'd gathered his bones and other relics from the four corners of the earth. You could hear the gasps, given that no one in the village barring the Norman overlords and maybe the odd mendicant friar has even ventured more than ten miles from the city walls.

He held up a tiny piece of wood.

'I have in my possession several splinters of our Redeemer's cross, carried by Saint Thomas on his travels through India,' he said.

'Where's India?' someone asked. It sounded like Stink's voice. I was pleased that someone else had spoken up, for I didn't wish to sound ignorant.

'It's that-a-way,' the pedlar said, and he pointed at the horizon. I thought about it and, by my reckoning, he was indicating that India's roughly north by north east of Exeter.

Stink then asked what India was like and I was pleased he'd asked that, too.

It's beautiful, the pedlar told us.

'It's as green as grass, it smells of perfume and spices and it's as warm as the sun, which shines there all day and all night,' he said.

'Do they have hexotic hanimals?' another man asked.

'Indeed, my friend,' the pedlar said, looking the man up and down. 'I've encountered cockatrices and basilisks and have even slain a fire-breathing dragon.'

'How did you haccomplish that?'

'I merely swallowed a draft of this elixir.' He held up a bottle. 'It endows you with the strength and courage of a lion and can even, in some well-documented cases, render a cripple whole again. Indeed my very own father lay abed with the palsy for many a year but, having drunk one swig of this for ten successive mornings before the cock crew, he rose again and now spends his days jigging merrily about the streets of the fair city of Bristol.'

Which is a quite miraculous thing.

As he spoke, he looked at us, each and every one. When he looked into my eyes, he smiled in a way no man had ever smiled at me before. In that moment, I felt as if it were just him and me there. As if we were the only two people in the whole world.

Then, when his eyes moved on, I still felt an afterglow inside me. A warmed pot stays warm, long after it's been removed from the fire. So it was with me.

I watched him as he concluded. His wasn't a beautiful face. Not like Eadwerd's, for example. Eadwerd is pretty enough to have been a girl. The pedlar was handsome, I'd say. It was his eyes that drew you to him. They burned with passion.

People were falling over themselves to buy his relics. One crippled man looked at him forlornly, because he had only a penny and not enough to buy a bottle of the elixir that might have cured his woes.

I held back. Partly to avoid all that jostling and shouting. Partly because I was shy about going up and asking for a splinter of the Redeemer's cross. I wanted the pedlar to speak to me but, at the same time I wanted to run away.

Yes, it's true. Love (or at least a certain dazzling, hit-you-like-a-lightning-flash type of love) makes you want to run a mile *and* stay rooted to spot. The only way this is possible is if love tears you apart. I was torn.

But I plucked up the courage. For a penny, it seemed a good idea to ensure an eternity of bliss in the afterlife. When I held out the coin and asked him for a piece of the cross, he grasped my hand and closed it, then whispered that I should keep my money.

'Why?' I asked him, flushing hotly, even though I knew why.

'Because,' he said, all quiet and calm and masterful, 'you're the loveliest thing I've ever beheld.'

I was struck mute.

I believe it was Stink, standing behind me, who leaned over and warned me that the pedlar would have said such honeyed words to many a maiden before me. Stink's words were intended not just for my ears, but the pedlar's, too.

'Maybe,' came the pedlar's reply, 'but I've never before meant them as I do now.'

The urge to fly gained dominion over me and I was running away, all dignity gone. That, I told myself, would be the end of that. A flame snuffed out as quickly as it's taken hold.

When I found Eadwerd and Robin again, Robin's love for the mermaid seemed to have been rekindled, although – according to Ed – she'd been evasive on the matter of marriage, looking at Robin wistfully and saying she doubted the legality of such an arrangement, though she didn't dismiss it entirely. She suggested that he might be advised to visit her a few more times to discuss matters further. In the light of this, she was prepared to agree to three visits for the price of two.

When I showed the splinter of the Redeemer's cross to Ed, I mentioned nothing of the pedlar's words. Ed took a look at it and declared that the Lord's cross was made of English Elm, which was a wonder. He also said that, though it must be more than a thousand years old, it looked as fresh and as sappy as newly-hewn wood, and the weevils had left it without the usual pockmarks.

'That's more than a wonder, Perty. It's an undeniable miracle,' he said.

As I carried it around with me, it was as if I carried a lover's kiss.

I was angry with Ed when he told Sunny I'd been given it without being charged. That made me feel – all of a sudden – as if I were in possession of a guilty secret.

Sunny put down his whistle.

'Show me, Perty,' he said.

He scrutinised it for a while, smiled indulgently, and then handed it back to me.

'What's up?' I asked. I can always tell when father wishes to shield me from something.

'Let me ask you a question, Perty, and then I'll tell you. Do you remember when the whistle told you that there are three ways in which a man might love you: with his head, with his heart and with his lips?'

'I can't speak for the whistle, but I remember when *you* told me that, father.'

'Don't allow yourself to fall for a man who whispers seductively in your ear, like the serpent in the Garden of Eden. Do you think yourself in love?'

'No, father,' I protested.

'Well, my whistle tells me otherwise. So beware, Perty. And yes, I'll tell you what you're holding. The whistle says it's what we call a genuine, indisputably-proven fake. It was given you not by a pedlar, but a rogue.'

I was tearful. For a fleeting moment I hated my father. But hate for the ones you love melts as quickly as ice does in the sun.

He put an arm around me.

'Between you and me, Perty,' he whispered, 'I think the whistle's got this one wrong. I reckon you're right to believe in miracles.'

He sighed a deep sigh and then he was off again.

Stories take your mind off the little worries that are in danger of nibbling away at you the way the wind nibbles away at a rock face.

VII

Talbot. According to Sunny, the very name means *doomsayer*. I've no reason to doubt him.

When Aunt Wilburh met and fell in love with Uncle Talbot, she'd imagined him to be a brooding poet as she'd looked at his dark, handsome features. She was only half right. Whilst poetry was probably lost on Talbot, he did an awful lot of brooding. He had that way of peering at you, too. Aunt Wilburh mistook it for some deep yearning on Talbot's part, the way he'd watched her intently from across the road as she'd walked off to fetch water from the well or logs from beyond the city walls. How was she to know that Talbot was peering at her the way he peered at everyone, because his eyes weren't exactly the best the Almighty could have granted a man.

Overcome by curiosity and being a wilful sort of girl, it was Wilburh who'd made the first move and spoken to Talbot, alone. Even suggested their first kiss.

'She was bashless,' Talbot chips in, interrupting Sunny. 'I was a bashful young lad and Wilburh was utterly without bash.'

'Nonsense,' Wilburh corrects Talbot. 'I just wasn't prepared to hang around for a lifetime while he sat on his fat arse. Although to be fair, it was a rather nice little arse back then.'

'Wilburh. Please. Not in front of the children,' Grandmother Edie says.

Sunny coughs.

'If the whistle and I might be allowed to continue . . .'

Wilburh had a torrent of questions. Who were his parents? Why did he keep peering at her? And so on.

Most of her questions were met with a shrug of his shoulders. Admittedly, she thought they were a good pair of shoulders that shrugged alluringly. There was also a lot to be said in favour of a boy who didn't say much. Such boys were less likely to answer back once you were wed and had to take control of things.

Besides. The past is dead and gone. A dark, brooding boy with a murky dead-and-gone past was much more exciting that a pallid boy with an unblemished past. Either way, history should be left to look after itself.

The past is little more than a dung heap. If you go rummaging in a midden, you're more likely to unearth the stench of shit than you are a sparkling diamond.

Osbert – the foundling whose genesis is shrouded in mystery – only ever delved into the past in the form of the books lying in the minster library, preferring to look to a future in which he'd have bettered himself. Sunny and his whistle, when not wallowing in the past, conjured prophesies about the future. But Wilburh – spirited, impulsive Wilburh – lived for the moment. Her life was in the sunlit or rained-upon present.

'Men and women,' Grandmother Edie explains. 'Women are concerned with what has to be done in the here-and-now, because no one else is going to prepare food or sweep floors. As for men, they assume food prepares itself and floors sweep themselves, while they daydream about a cherished past or a longed-for future.'

'I wish you'd warned me about men before I became wedded to Talbot,' Wilburh sighs.

According to Aunt Wilburh, you marry a boy because he's young, brooding and handsome. When youth and handsomeness desert him, he remains brooding. Though Wilburh acknowledges there's something to be said for having a husband such as Talbot. From the outset, they slowly sap the excitement from your married life. As opposed to the sort of man who'll bring you crashing back to earth if your dreams and hopes head too far skywards. That sort makes for a bad husband.

I believe this is called *managing your expectations.*

VIII

When the pedlar had first looked into my eyes, I didn't know which way to turn or which way to look. Anywhere but into his eyes. It reminded me of those moments after you look at the sun and have to avert your gaze and everywhere you turn, there are hundreds of green apples dancing in your head. Only, this time it wasn't apples I saw: it was his face, and the dancing was not in my head so much as in the very pit of my being. My heart was drumming away, all frit and excited.

A new day. I was walking around the stalls, feigning interest, but secretly hoping I might see the pedlar. I wanted him to talk about the places he'd seen and I wanted to ask him why he'd chosen me, though I knew I wouldn't dare to, because this would be *forward*. Aunt Wilburh might have known how to ensnare Uncle Talbot, but I'm not forward. In fact, in such matters, I'm backward.

Grandfather Aart and Sunny both say I've always had what they call *spirit*, but this is something different. Spirit is standing up for Eadwerd when he was being bullied or giving someone a piece of my mind if they were being cruel to one of the Almighty's creatures. Spirit is having the will to tell Uncle Osbert that I'd chosen to decline his proposal that we should be wed.

But spirit flies out of you when a man looks into your eyes and speaks of love. When spirit leaves your body, you go weak at the knees and your stomach becomes knotted.

I went to the tree, but he wasn't there and I began thinking that maybe my father's whistle was right for divining that my piece of cross and my pedlar were fakes, both. Then I heard his voice behind me.

'You've come,' he said and – all over again – I didn't know whether to run or to stay.

'Yes,' I said, having wanted to say something along the lines that I just happened to be idling. Except that I was flustered, so no such words came.

'Bernard,' he said, in his bewitching way.

I wallowed in the word. *Bear-nar*, he pronounced it, the gentle ending of the word almost – but not quite – forming into a *d*, which would have been harder on the ear and more akin to my own way of speaking.

He offered me his hand, all formal, and he whispered, as he did so, that it would be a fine thing to wrap me in his arms. '. . . though that would never do, on first acquaintance,' he added.

'No,' I agreed.

'I wouldn't want to frighten you away,' he said.

Then he asked me my name.

'Perty,' I replied, and he said it was the most beautiful name for a beautiful maiden.

Slowly, I felt some of the spirit return to me and I found I could say more than one word at a time. I wanted to know all about him and where he'd travelled. Any place I mentioned, he'd been there.

'Is Africa as hot as they say?' I asked him.

'It's as hot as the blood that flows through you and me,' he said. 'The skies are bigger there and the stars brighter, the sands are endless and the people are so fried by the sun that they're burned to black.'

'And what of Bristol?' I asked him.

'A mite wetter and cooler than Africa,' he said.

'And where is your home?'

'I have none, Perty. These feet of mine will never stand still.'

'Where were you born?'

'Normandy,' he said. 'Which is like Devon, here, in more ways than you might suppose. For years, we've had to endure tribulations. Duke William's sons fighting for control of the place. As ever, it's we peasants who have to bear the brunt. Taxes. Trying to work out who your real lord and master is. The trick is to take sides against the one who's likely to punish you slightly less if he wins. This is what they call *hedging your bets*.'

'So why are you so far from your birthplace?'

'Better to be a Norman in England than a Norman in Normandy. If I ladle on my French accent here, slip some pennies into the hands of his Lordship's henchmen, wherever I sell my wares, I'm left alone. If I have no home, they have no home to burn to the ground. Such is the easy come and easy go life of the pedlar.'

I was seated on the ground now and he was lying on his side, propped up on his right arm, his fist tucked under his chin, never taking his eyes off me, and chewing on a blade of grass. He told me he'd seen probably every girl who ever walked God's earth, but that I was the loveliest. I knew this was what they call *sweet talk* or *honeyed words*, because if ears could taste, then such words would be as nectar. And though I knew I should be wary of believing a single utterance of his, that didn't stop me from feeling a swell of excitement as he spoke his fine words.

I wanted to ask him why he thought me beautiful, but that would have shown forwardness, not spiritedness.

'I must sell some of my wares,' he said, finally, standing up and dusting himself down. 'All this lying down beside my sweetheart will impoverish me.'

My heart leapt when he called me his *sweetheart*.

'I should like to see you at dusk, Perty,' he said. 'Then I can kiss those lips of yours with no fear of a rebuke from that madman with the cur or any others who would decry me.'

I felt a sudden surge of shame wash over me, for he was recalling the moment last year when Uncle Osbert and Dog had both been barking their protestations at those they termed charlatans, though I reckon Dog was merely following Osbert's lead.

'I'll see,' I said. But I knew it was as if I were already rolling or running down a slope and there was nothing I could do to stop myself, even if I were to try.

'The whistle has been giving me shrill warnings all day, Perty,' my father greeted me, when I arrived home. 'It talks of a man with itchy feet. It tells me there are two reasons a man will keep walking and never stand still for more than a week or so. The first reason is this. A man might have an end in mind. He might dream of untold wealth or a better life beyond the here-and-now. He'll keep running towards that future dream. The second reason a man might have itchy feet is this. He's running from some murky secrets in his past. He might even be evading the reach of the law. Beware, Perty. The whistle speaks of a man from afar who runs both from his past and to his future.'

Uncle Osbert was listening in.

'Perty's already proved herself a match for any suitor,' he said. I felt he said it with admiration, not bitterness.

'True, Ossie. But her judgement's never previously been clouded by something we call *lovestruckness*. He might be a wise old owl, our Ossie, but he lacks the wit to woo,' Sunny quipped.

He sounded a screech and a ghostly too-woo on his pipe. There's a time and place for humour. This wasn't it.

That barb must have hurt Uncle Osbert more than he let on. I could see the pain in his eyes on being told he couldn't engender feelings of abandon in a girl. I wanted to tell him that I *did* love him, but in the way I loved my father and the rest of my family. With tenderness, not with passion.

Sometimes I curse my father Sunny's whistle for the pain it spreads. It never knows when to keep its counsel. Sometimes we need words and music in our lives. Sometimes we need silence, the chance to listen to the unspoken word and the unplayed melody.

Uncle Talbot leaned over.

'Someone should stick that blasted whistle up the dark recesses of your father's rear end.'

'I imagine Sunny would still manage to pipe some tune or other, even then,' Aunt Wilburh said. 'It's sometimes called *whistling in the dark*. Other people called it *talking through your arse*. I call it *a lot of hot air.*'

Osbert's lip curled into a half-smile. Since they'd been young, Wilburh had been the one who'd had to come to his defence with some witty riposte or other.

'Less squabbling, please,' Grandmother Edie said.

'Quite right,' Uncle Talbot said. 'My veins are swelling up with all this bickering. Who'd like to massage my legs?'

Unsurprisingly, there were no takers.

'Oh well,' Talbot said. 'I'll just have to massage myself.'

He began unstrapping his leggings.

IX

While Talbot massaged his swollen veins, dulling the pain, Sunny picked up the thread of his story. Storytelling's perhaps not too far removed from massaging swollen veins. It's probably another way of dulling pain.

Although largely preoccupied with the present – with chores – Wilburh allowed herself the occasional dream. In particular, she allowed herself to imagine brighter-than-the-present futures for each of her offspring: all ten of them.

Talbot, being a doommonger had peered at each of them and warned her – with uncanny accuracy – that none of them would survive for long. Nine times out of ten, he was right. Only Cousin Robin – too dumb to read the script Fate had written – proved him wrong.

'He might be as miserable as a cold, wet February and he might be useless in most respects, but your Uncle Talbot at least stopped me from getting ideas above my station,' Aunt Wilburh whispered to me.

My father, Sunny, had been little more than a boy when Wilburh and Talbot had declared that they were to be wed and that Talbot would be moving into the one-roomed house with Aart, Edie and their brood of three.

'What do you reckon?' Wilburh had asked, seizing the moment by the scruff of its neck.

Talbot had shrugged his shoulders and peered at her. He'd looked quite pleased with himself. She'd taken that as a 'yes'.

As is often the case, their first night together had involved some inept fumbling.

'I can't. Not in front of everyone,' Talbot had whispered.

'It's dark. No one's watching,' Wilburh had said, quietly.

'For heaven's sake,' Grandmother Edie had said. 'Can you two get on with it, so that we can all sleep?'

'Apologies, mother-in-law,' Talbot had said. 'This isn't easy.'

'Sunny,' Grandfather Aart had said. 'Give us all a tune on your whistle, to calm Talbot's frayed nerves and give us something else to listen to while they do what they have to.'

Sunny had played a mellifluous, seductive tune that could have charmed a snake and then he overlaid that with a rhythmic second movement. Capped it all off with a rousing finale.

'Well done, Sunny,' Grandfather Aart had said. 'That was just what the doctor ordered.'

'Well done, Talbot,' Grandmother Edie had added. 'Shall we all sleep now?'

Unseen in the darkness, Osbert had no doubt curled his lip in disgust.

But now it's my turn to be cursed by sleeplessness.

Whatever Sunny and his whistle might say, I know one thing. If I haven't met Bernard again before the sun sets tomorrow and if he leaves before he's held me in his arms, then I'll weep with anguish. If I lie with him and then he leaves me, I'll weep with anguish, too.

The Holy Bible teaches us that the wages of sin is death. So said Uncle Osbert in one of his lessons. What neither the Bible nor Uncle Osbert told me was that the wages of being in love is torment. Perhaps Uncle Osbert and the scribes who penned the Bible knew a lot about sin but they didn't know what it feels like to be in love.

X

In the morning, my mind was elsewhere than in the present. I fed the animals in the castle courtyard, though, for all I know, the geese were fed the hay and the cows given grain. I spoke merrily enough with those who greeted me, but I could tell you neither the words they said nor the replies I gave.

My chores done, I mingled with the crowds. Finally, when the noise of the fair began to abate, and when the merchants started to pack up their wares and, grasping their pennies, make their way to the alehouses, I waited for Bernard beneath our tree.

When I saw him coming my way, my heart leaped.

He said nothing at first, but held me and, before I knew it, he had his arms around me and was kissing me as no man had ever done before. It was the closest I'd ever come to feeling I was flying.

There was urgency in his voice when he finally spoke.

'I want to claim you for my own, Perty,' he said. 'A life spent travelling is no life for a girl. No. When I've made my fortune, I'll return and make you my wife and we shall live together wherever you wish. Here or in India or Africa or Bristol. We'll grow old together, you and I. But, in the meantime, if you are to be my wife, then you must show me you love your Bernard like no other.'

'We must show patience,' I pleaded with him.

'Why?' he asked.

'I barely know you,' I said. 'Nor you me. We have a lifetime to look forward to. Besides, I could come with you, if you wish. I could sew and cook and read and write for you.'

'Read and write?' he asked. 'Why in God's name would I want you to read and write for me? It's your love I seek.'

'Besides,' I said. Then my voice tailed off, for I was thinking two thoughts.

The first was that my mother had died in giving birth to me. What if he were to leave me with child? Would the same not happen to me? Would my life not be snuffed out as surely as my mother's was? And who would care for my bairn, because my family would believe a child so born to be the spawn of the very devil and Bernard would be tramping the earth and selling his relics and nowhere at hand to help.

My second thought was that maybe Uncle Osbert and Sunny and the whistle were right. Perhaps the splinter of cross and Bernard were one and the same. Fakes.

I told him that what we were doing wasn't right. Neither in the eyes of the Almighty, nor in the eyes of anyone else but him. Kissing can lead to the making of bairns, I said. And delivering a baby into this world was what killed my mother.

'I'll never go killing you with any bairns of mine,' Bernard said, 'for I'm blessed with what they call *the luck of the Normans*. The Almighty blessed our race at Hastings. Then He blessed me by giving me the gift of the fragments of the Redeemer's cross. He blessed me when He led me to the arms of my Perty and He shall bless me by giving me a fortune and making Perty my beloved wife. So I can tell you, as surely as I can tell you the sun will set each day and then rise again in the morning: our bairns will bring you the blessings of joy, not the curse of death.'

He sat down.

'Come,' he beckoned me towards him, and I did as I was bidden, though I was cautious. Not forward.

He kissed me again as I lay there beside him. Then I was

aware of his fumbling hungrily inside my skirts and I feared I was his completely.

I knew, now, why they called it *fallen*. When you're kissed by a man you love, when a man would make love to you and your resistance is gone, then this is like falling from a great height. You cannot hang on or slow your fall, once you've leaped. There's no undoing what's done. A fallen maiden cannot the next day be unfallen. A maiden deflowered cannot be a maiden ever again.

Even in that moment – with my head swarming with all the advice I'd ever heard in my life and all of it contradictory – I swear I heard the faint, plaintive note of my father Sunny's whistle, summoning me to my senses.

It was late. I should be gone.

'I have to help prepare my father's supper,' I said, sitting up. It was a lie, because Grandmother Edie and Aunt Wilburh were the ones who cooked for us all most nights, though, more often than not, I'd stand beside them, watching, learning and helping.

'Your Bernard's not yet sated,' he said. He wanted more and grasped me firmly by my wrists and told me not to leave him.

'If you love me, you'll let me go,' I said, showing spirit.

He kissed me again with passion. I had to pull away.

'Fate has decreed we should be lovers,' he said. 'Fate gives not a finch's fart for your father and his blasted supper.'

I felt we were being watched. You know when you're being watched, though don't ask me how. Perhaps the Almighty was watching over me, a sinner. Perhaps it was Robin or some other boy, spying on me.

I looked around, anxiously. He sensed the same.

'I love you like no other, though,' I said, rising to my feet.

XI

'The course of true love never runs smoothly, Perty,' Aunt Wilburh said. 'Normally it meanders this way and that, like a great river on a flood plain. Though in your Uncle Talbot's case it was more of a dribble than a flow. More of a leaky pipe dripping into a culvert.'

She was right about the meanders of love. For every heart-pounding measure of excitement, there's an equal and equivalent weight of gloom.

That which rises must also come back down to earth.

Day and night.

Summer and winter.

After our meal, the three of us – Eadwerd, Robin and I – ventured out into the evening air. Picking up their stems of plantain, Ed and Robin played a half-hearted game of swordsmen.

'I, sire, shall fight for my beloved sister,' Ed announced, mimicking the accent of a well-bred Norman knight.

'I know for a fact Perty's a fallen woman,' Robin said.

'You're full of more shit than a midden,' Ed accused him, less knightly than before.

'Look,' Robin persisted. 'She's blushing and that's proof enough.

'Liar,' Eadwerd said and he boxed Robin's right ear. Then he turned to me.

'He's lying, is he, Perty?'

'Only half, though I'd rather not speak of these things.'

'Well you've had one ear boxed for telling half a lie and I'll spare you the other ear and call it quits,' Eadwerd said. Then he looked at me again.

'You know, Perty. You can always speak to me and I'd not let it spill to a single soul.'

'I know, Ed,' I replied and I began weeping. 'Leave us,' he said to Robin, but Robin was in no mood to let go.

'Why?' he asked.

'Because,' Ed hesitated. 'Because I saw that mermaid and she said she was trying to find you so she could plan your wedding.'

'Where was she?' he asked, excitedly.

'About a mile down the River Exe. She said you needed to be quick or she'd swim off to sea.'

Robin was off and Ed and I started giggling. I think it was my way of letting all my worries come tumbling out.

I told Ed everything. How Bernard had whispered sweet talk and how he'd felt me in places he shouldn't have, but I'd only let him because we were to be man and wife when he'd made his fortune.

'Do you think he's a fake, Ed?'

'I can't know one way or another, Perty. But if he is, I'll box both his ears and twice as hard as I've ever boxed Robin's.'

'You can't do that, Ed.'

'Why not?'

'Because he's a Norman. You can't go hitting a Norman. Not even a Norman peasant. You'd have your hand cut off.'

'I wouldn't mind that one bit, Perty. Not if it righted a wrong.'

'And how would you carve with only one hand?'

'Badly, I reckon.'

We were giggling again.

I believe that where love sometimes hurts and sometimes has you welling up with joy, laughter is only ever wondrous.

If I were the Almighty, I'd not have made all the streets of heaven paved with gold and all that other nonsense. If you're there for eternity, the excitement of all that gold would wear off soon enough. So I'd have made heaven full of laughter, instead.

Laughter's the one thing you could put up with for eternity and never grow bored with it.

XII

The following evening, I'd not seen Bernard. My heart was aching. Eadwerd was late coming home and I was wondering what excuse I could glean to slip away, particularly since Robin was likely to stir up trouble. Not through any malice, but through mere stupidity. I feared all sorts of outcomes. Not least Ed being set upon by the band of travellers if he'd tried to hand out a beating to Bernard.

'She's gone,' Robin was muttering about his mermaid. 'You and Ed should have warned me earlier, Perty.'

'Not to worry, Robin,' Sunny said. 'She'll not have swum far.'

Then I was imagining another outcome. Bernard's gone, I was thinking. That was when Eadwerd arrived, all hot and bothered.

Sunny picked up his whistle and played it quietly. He looked up.

'The whistle informs me Ed has something he wishes to tell you, Perty. But I, as your father, say that he should share it with the rest of us. A family that shares its darkest secrets is all the stronger for it. Besides, only the four of us are here right now. Robin. Leave us, please.'

'Why? I like dark secrets.'

'Because you prefer mermaids to dark secrets and I just saw that mermaid of yours up in the main square.'

'Why didn't you tell me, Uncle Sunny?' he asked. Then he was off.

Ed revealed that he'd seen Bernard outside an inn.

'Supping beer from his illgotten gains and joking about how he'd helped himself to a tasty maiden. Bragging about how he was going to feast right royally on her tonight. I should have said nothing but I walked up to him too brave for my own good and called him a liar for saying Perty was a fornicator. "Liar?" says he. "Then ask your pretty sister this. Ask her if she'd like to make babies with her Bernard and to be his wife. You tell her that her Bernard shall wed her when he's made his fortune."'

Eadwerd looked up at me. Sunny said nothing.

'I was so cross,' Ed continued. 'I could have wrung his scrawny neck but I thought he might be telling the truth in saying you were to be man and wife.'

'Tell me the truth, Perty,' Father said. 'Are you fallen?'

I was sobbing and unable to speak up. Eadwerd spoke for me.

'Perty's not fallen,' he said. 'She was only kissed.'

I was grateful to Ed for not mentioning that I'd been touched beneath my skirts.

'Well done, then, Perty. You've shown spirit,' Sunny said, placing an arm around my shoulder. 'You're not the first maiden to have been duped by a fox and I don't suppose you'll be the last. Maybe we should all have listened to Ossie. He's no fool. He said they were not to be trusted. Maybe you should have agreed to wed your Uncle Osbert and then there'd have been none of this trouble.'

'I don't love Uncle Ossie as a man and nor could I ever, for he's all words and numbers and feels no love.'

'Ah, but he means well.'

'Don't listen to Father. He's only jesting,' Ed said and then I saw Sunny was smiling.

I began crying again, so Sunny let up.

'I'll never leave you, Perty,' he said.

'Nor I,' Eadwerd said. 'I'd stand by you in any storm, Perty.'

'Aye,' Sunny said. 'Ed, too. Ed will never leave you.'

Robin had appeared at the door.

'The mermaid's slipped from my grasp again,' he said, dejectedly.

'That'll be on account of the scaly skin on that tail of hers. Very tricky indeed to grasp,' Sunny said and, raising his whistle to his lips, he played a melody that conjured rolling waves and the sinuous stroke of a mermaid swimming.

'Ah, love,' he sighed, when he was done. 'Why does it hurt us so?' Then he promised us a story, plucked from the family's distant past. To take our minds off our present sorrows.

'I think an eventful tale's called for,' he said. 'A story about turning points.'

XIII

It takes one spark to light the flame. It always does.

This is the spark that kindled the flame that lit the candle that, falling, fuelled the fire that begat the blaze that fed the inferno that consumed the house that Pimp built. Leaving it no longer a home, reducing it to a smouldering heap of charcoal. And while the flames had spat and cackled, they'd cursed Pimp and they'd cursed the Shrike. They'd snarled angrily at their two drunken, snoring forms.

Sunny was the first to spot the smoke billowing through the thatch, though none of them could work out which of the warren of rooms it was coming from. Sunny took the whistle to his lips and summoned rain, but the Almighty sent wind instead. Yes, and what is it that snuffs out a candle but ushers in a fire? It's the riddling, contrary wind that blows where it wills and answers to no man.

People were running from Pimp's house, many of them clutching their clothes. An angel of mercy – seeking redemption – had risked her own life by unlocking every bedroom door. Ten girls in a state of disarray and ten husbands, though admittedly not husbands to these particular girls. They emerged, in pairs, the men looking about themselves anxiously, when you'd have thought relief at having escaped might be their foremost emotion. In two cases, their anxiety proved justified. Their wives had spotted them. When relief had subsided and the glow of the embers had died, there would be hell to pay. Fiery hot scoldings followed by a cooling of relations.

Wan and Tway, deep in the furthest depths of the warren of rooms, weren't accounted for. Nor were Pimp and Nell.

Tway would never be able to tell anyone what had happened. Because Tway was mute. She'd always sat, silently, while Sunny – seated there in their cell and falling deeper in love – had teased stories, word by reluctant word, from Wan. Tway was mute. Which was why she'd been chosen and why the fire had come, breathing vengeance.

Talbot arrived, panting, at the scene.

'Follow me,' Sunny said and he and Talbot charged into the burning, smoke-filled house.

'Wan,' Sunny shouted, repeatedly.

He heard her, whimpering. He and Talbot gasped for air. The house was groaning with pain as the flames engulfed it. Held fast in Sunny's belt, the whistle heard what the people couldn't. It heard the house screaming for water.

'Tway,' was all Wan said as she pointed to the next room.

'I'll go,' Talbot said to Sunny. 'You take Wan.'

Talbot burrowed into the smoke, like a mole tunnelling through the dark earth. Perhaps he tells the truth when he claims he was a mole in his previous, happier life.

Sunny and Wan emerged first. Talbot and Tway soon afterwards.

But Talbot then turned immediately back into the house again. It was as if he'd been living a life of indolence awaiting this moment. Storing up his resources – his energy and resolve – for this moment of bravery, though some would call it *foolhardiness*.

Once he emerges, he'll be free to enjoy a life of unbroken indolence again. His sins of apathy and bone idleness will be forgiven.

As Tway lay there, her eyes were dead and her mouth as mute as ever. But she was alive. And any life, however miserable, must surely be better than death.

Tway had been as weightless as light itself, as Talbot had carried her bruised body, darkening where she'd been struck, otherwise as pale as the moon. But this second body Talbot carried was a heavy one, burdened, as it was, by a lifetime's worth of sin, though not much in the way of guilt.

Sin is heavier even than lead.

Talbot had been gone too long. Wilburh was beside herself, wailing.

'Foolish man. Why did he have to go back in?'

She was pregnant, carrying Talbot's child. This was the tenth time his seed had grown in her. Nine times, Talbot – in that despondent way of his – had told her that the child inside her was doomed. Because it was his. Nine times, he'd been proved correct: her offspring had barely seen the light of day. Robin would defy the odds, of course. Rules and reason being beyond his numbskull's brain.

The fire was crackling greedily and they'd all just heard another beam come crashing to the ground. So what possessed Talbot to enter the burning house again? Perhaps a life spent obeying orders is the best explanation. Because it's the lot of all Englishmen to do as they're told by their masters, never to step out of line, but to form an orderly queue. Always to *do the right thing*. Yes, perhaps Talbot was simply being thoroughly English.

He was stumbling, as opposed to burrowing purposefully, now. But he peered, unseeing, into the smoke, as any self-respecting mole might and he tunnelled his way to where his twitching snout was telling him to go. He found the person he was searching for; not where he left them, but staggering, drunk on smoke and wine. An utterly lost soul.

Talbot grabbed him by the wrist. Ignored his yelps of pain, as yet unaware that the charred timber that had roused the man from his sleep had left a mark across his face and chest. Oblivious, too, to the fact that the man was as naked as a newborn.

Of the two, only Talbot heard Sunny's whistle. Sunny had gained his breath again and he was guiding Talbot to where he must burrow, blindly. There was a breathless shriek of desperation about the whistle.

But emerge they did. Wilburh fell to her knees and kissed Talbot repeatedly as if making up for all those times she snapped at him. Talbot had tunnelled his way to redemption.

Pimp and Nell were still in there, trapped in their own hell. Sinful, scarlet Pimp and Nell. Consumed by the red-hot fire. Beyond saving. Even Sunny's whistle maintained a dignified silence, as if to acknowledge this.

Pimp's girls seemed terrified by their sudden freedom. As preyed-upon animals might feel in an exposed space. Wan and Tway were also unable to bear the light assailing them. Grandmother Edie covered their eyes with improvised linen hoods. When you've been trapped in a dark room for most of your life, the brightness is too much. You can't bear to see the light.

And another thing. When you're kept in the dark, the blindingly obvious eludes you. As will become apparent, when Wilburh and Edie will have to teach the two girls – their new cause – the most basic of skills, such as how to heat pottage, how to stir it, how to wash their hands and much, much more.

But the most important lesson they must learn is the same skill that Dog will have to spend so long trying to teach Osbert some years hence.

The art of allowing yourself to be loved.

XIV

Neither the Shrike nor the Almighty holds much store by atonement. Vengeance is more their thing. They leave talk of redemption or forgiveness to the Galilean and his followers.

But this much was sure. The Shrike had paid for his many sins with a deep scar that ran across his face and body. Pimp and Nell had paid a greater price.

The twelve girls were free. Wan and Tway and the other ten. But they all, in their different ways, feared the freedom they'd craved.

The cathedral church is able to offer the homeless four things: a roof over their heads, food to sustain them, much compassion to nurture them, and liberation, a slate wiped clean.

You're ill advised to grasp freedom with both hands. Better to welcome it with guarded caution. Better to learn to stand before you learn to walk before you learn to run before you learn to fly. None of the girls is able to throw their chains aside.

Where would they go? The men who were glad enough to part with their silver to lie with them while they were imprisoned would run a mile from them, now. Who will take a freed whore and make her his wife? Only the most gracious of men and they're in short supply. Most of them have already been snaffled up.

The church stepped forward and offered them – the girls and Aart's family – a bed for each of them to lie on. At times such as this, even Sunny and Talbot were prepared to concede that the church is a good thing.

'Like a tallow candle,' Talbot observes. 'The church sheds light in dark places but sometimes gives off a fearful stench.'

For once, there was unequivocally a warm glow emanating from the place.

Seated in the very same building where his mother and father were raised, Sunny picked up his whistle. And from it, he teased a story.

The whistle told how Pimp, his pockets lined with silver after a most satisfying transaction, had been supping some of the finest wine he could get his chubby hands on and was on the cusp of a drunken stupor. Nell, having merely allowed the faint shadow of disapproval to cloud her features for a fleeting moment, had earned a thrashing. Before he'd passed out, Pimp had sent her reeling, staggering across the room. As she'd crashed against the table, the one at which he counted his illgotten winnings as assiduously as any shepherd would count his sheep, the candle had toppled over and on to the rush floor.

Her arm had been in such pain she thought Pimp must have broken it. Her first thought, as she saw that the flames had caught, was to free the girls. She'd raised the alarm, and with her left hand – because her right hand had refused to obey her or to offer any assistance – she'd unlocked any locked doors. Wan's had been the last room to be unlocked. Wan had been alone. Tway had lain in the next room. This, Nell had understood now, was why Pimp's coffers had been so full to bursting. The first of his two most prized assets had been sold to the highest bidder.

Wan had refused to move. There had been no time to argue with her. Nell had heard the young piper advancing to the room. She'd leave it to him to save Wan and Tway. She'd fought her way back through the smoke-filled corridors until she'd reached the room in which Pimp had been lying, drunk on the floor. The smoke had been so thick and the flames so hot that he couldn't possibly have survived. But, just to be sure, she'd checked, and the door had still been firmly locked. Her work completed, she'd slumped against the door. At the very gates of hell. She'd winced as she'd caught her right arm against the wooden jamb. It was over now. The pain would soon be in the past. So said the whistle.

Osbert rolled his eyes, choosing to disbelieve all that nonsense about the whistle and what it said to his younger brother. Any fool, sifting through the charred remains of their house could have seen that the lock, rendered unusable by the heat of the fire but still intact, unlike the oak door it had once graced, was still in a bolted position. Any fool could have bent down, inspected Nell's burnt corpse and seen the way the bone of her right arm had been severed just above the wrist.

Why are all these people beguiled by his idiot brother Sunny's tales, he wonders. Why are they not more concerned with facts?

XV

Aart ventured from the cathedral to visit the Shrike.

He flinched as he looked at the open wound, scarring his master's face.

'A Lord is never beholden to his vassal,' the Shrike whispered, hoarsely. 'Nevertheless I'm grateful to you and your kin, Aart. By way of thanks, I'll grant you any wish.'

'My only wish, maistre, is that I might be allowed to continue serving you by providing you with the unadulterated truth.'

'Yes, yes. Enough of that. I demand a wish worthy of the name.'

'Perhaps that my son, Osbert, an earnest boy who's studied the trivium and shown a pleasing level of accomplishment in understanding and scribing Latin, might assist me in serving you. And that you might also see fit to allow my third-born, Sunngifu, to take the hand of the maiden Wan in marriage and that you might forego any claim to her. And that you might consent to Edie's and my treating the other girl, Tway, as our own daughter.'

'These are four wishes.'

'Then my one wish is that you grant me four wishes, maistre.'

'Clever, Aart. Artful indeed.

'So, you are asking me to forgo my *jus primae noctis*, my right to deflower the delectable waif, whom the late, unlamented Pimp has primed for my pleasure for God knows how many years?'

'This is my wish, maistre.'

'Very well. There are maidens aplenty in this crowded place. What of Osbert? Does he not wish to marry some woman?'

'I fear not, maistre. Osbert seems wedded to the written word. He shows no interest in matters of the flesh.'

'A strange boy.'

'Indeed, maistre.'

'Very well. Your wishes are all granted. Osbert shall work for me. If he proves himself as worthy as his father, he may even rise to become my Overseer of the Works at some future date. I shall need his unerring eye for detail as we rebuild those parts of the city the fire has claimed.'

They were interrupted.

'The doctor has arrived,' a servant announced.

'I thank you, maistre,' Aart said, as he shaped to leave.

'Stay, Aart,' the Shrike instructed him. 'See what this scoundrel has to say for himself. You, with your eagle's eye for distinguishing truth from falsehood.'

'Urine,' the doctor demanded, imperiously. 'A vial of my patient's urine.'

He handed the vessel to Aart.

'Urine?' Aart asked.

'I have spoken.'

'Maistre?' Aart asked the Shrike, tentatively.

'Very well. Help me, Aart.'

The Shrike turned awkwardly as Aart held the vial in place, turning his head away. The Shrike winced, attempted to summon the urine, but it was proving stubborn or bashful, unprepared to show its golden face to the world.

'Urine,' the doctor sounded forth, by way of distraction. 'As the great Notker has taught us, a small sample of urine can tell us all we wish to know.'

'What of my master's wounded flesh?' Aart asked. 'Does that not tell the story more vividly than a bottle of piss?'

'Piss?' the doctor scowled. 'A doctor does not inspect piss. Only the lowly piss. Only those unable to afford the services of a doctor. An overlord secretes liquid waste of a higher order.'

'Trust him,' the Shrike groaned, as urine finally flowed. 'He's a doctor.'

Aart handed over the vial. The doctor held it up to the light.

'A good golden colour,' he purred.

Then he held the vial to his nostrils and sniffed exaggeratedly.

'Ah,' he sighed. 'A most excellent odour. The urine of a fine, fit, healthy man with a voracious appetite for food, for drink, for women and for life. A man well equipped to recover from his wounds . . . though I must warn his Lordship he'll be left with scars, the evidence of his courage, a lasting badge of his honour.'

Aart rolled his eyes.

'I shall treat his Lordship's wounds with a poultice, to speed the process of healing. Thereafter, we must apply various unguents as I direct, while the scars are allowed to form. As for the pain, there is no better cure that the finest red wine. All will be well. So says your urine.'

'And how much will this cost me, given that it is my own urine that has been so eloquent and incisive?' the Shrike asked.

'Who can put a price on a lifetime's expertise?' the doctor responded.

'How much?'

Their visitor hesitated.

'Eight pence, my Lord.'

Aart raised his eyebrows. This was truly called *taking the piss*.

'Excellent. Give the man eight pennies.' The Shrike gestured towards his metal coffer. Aart remained astonished. Perhaps his master had lost his resolve in the conflagration.

Accepting the money, the doctor bowed obsequiously and backed out of the room.

'Very generous, maistre,' Aart observed.

'By which you mean *very foolish*, Aart. The truth, remember. Always the truth. We'll need to raise taxes if we're to get started on this building work. Ask Osbert, as his first task in my employ, to draw up a list of every tax payer and the burden we must place on them. Beside the good doctor's name, he should add a further eight pence. No. Make that nine pence for having made me suffer the indignity of pissing in front of him.'

'I can truthfully say that's an excellent suggestion, maistre.'

'Vials of urine and bottled truths,' Sunny scoffs. 'A man who believes he's found the absolute truth – the one and only way – is as big a fool as the one who says he can bottle the wind and rain. Once you've claimed the wind and rain, once you've entrapped them, they're diminished. They become mere air or water. A bottled truth, claimed as your own, is truth diminished. Truth must be allowed to run free. It must be strong and fit enough to be challenged. It mustn't be tethered or moulded to serve a man's needs. It must be allowed to run amok as wildly and as freely as the wind. The truth shall set you free. But only if the truth itself is free.'

XXVI

Sunny's stories. Of fire and water. Of events so many years ago. They're a distraction. But they can't entirely mask the truth of the here-and-now.

The merchants, the charlatans and the rest brought us relics, hope, entertainment and all manner of strange sights and sounds. They brought fleeting colour and joy into our dull lives. And now they're gone. It's as if the stalls and tents had never been there. We'll all have to return to grey reality and hard graft in place of falsehoods and fleeting dreams.

Bernard has gone, along with the rest of them. He's slipped away in the night. Foolish though I know it might be, I would have flown with him. But that was denied me. Perhaps someone – maybe Ed, Sunny or even Grandfather Aart – warned him not to come for me. The gossipmongers' tongues are all wagging. About who did what to whom. About which maiden lost her honour. It seems I'm not alone in being so maligned.

And now I hear that it's not only my honour that they took with them to their next fair, along the coast at Lyme. They've helped themselves to other chattels, too.

Uncle Osbert is still railing against them, even though they're miles beyond earshot.

'Those wolves, those vipers, those foxes. They've taken my cur away. Just when I'd grown fond of the beast. My spirits are at a low ebb. I've offered the hand of marriage and been spurned and now a cur has been wrested from me by a group of itinerant scoundrels. The beast has chosen to succumb to the temptation of a life of travel ahead of the company of an upright, God-fearing clerk.'

'When you put it like that, Ossie . . .' Sunny said.

Osbert was clenching and unclenching his fists. It would have been kinder to have left him to simmer down. Not to add to the heat. But Sunny spoke up.

'Would you like me to summon Dog with my whistle? It has remarkable powers, does this little wooden wonder.'

'You and your whistle can both go to hell,' Osbert shouted.

'Please, you two,' Grandmother Edie intervened. 'Sunny. Let things rest. I should have thought you have enough concerns of your own. People in timber houses shouldn't go kindling bonfires.'

Sunny placed the whistle to his lips and piped what seemed to be a soothing melody, to calm frayed nerves, including his own.

'Indeed,' Osbert said, refusing to yield. 'As you will have heard, certain maidens have been ravaged by the wastrels who descended upon us. They have stolen the innocence of more than one girl as surely as they have stolen my cur.'

'Perty isn't fallen,' Eadwerd spoke up. 'She wasn't ravished properly. Only touched in inappropriate places, which doesn't count as fornication, for all that that fox of a pedlar wanted it otherwise.'

Eadwerd turned to me.

'You've not fallen, Perty,' he said. 'You've just taken a stumble.'

'Well,' Grandfather Aart said. 'I reckon all of us could do with a brisk walk. Get a sniff of that wondrous stench of the city. Sunny. Grab that whistle and show us the way.'

Eadwerd held my hand as we walked.

'If Bernard were like you, he'd have wanted marriage over fornication,' I said.

'Well, he's nothing like me,' Eadwerd said. 'We're as different as foxes and lambs are, though – lamb or no lamb – I'd give him his comeuppance if he ever laid another finger on you, Perty. Then I'd march him to the late Seigneur's firstborn and request that he be birched and strung up by his balls.'

'That doesn't sound like a lamb talking,' I said.

I kissed his cheek; it was the kiss of a sister and brother, the best of friends. I wanted to tell Ed that I couldn't help myself. That I still loved Bernard as much as I did the first time he ever looked at me, beneath that tree.

'God help me to stop loving him,' I said.

Part Three

HEART

I

Land and stone. Sunny says the church and the Normans have laid claim to them both. You might assume the church would want to claim the moral high ground, he says. And indeed it often does. The church wants to reach up closer to the God whom they can never see and never touch, though they imagine He's somewhere up in the sky. It does this by building tall towers. It clamours for the Almighty's attention, in the way a wide-gaped nestling clamours for its parents' food. The church hopes that the Almighty will answer the prayers that reach Him first, the prayers that have less far to travel in the wind. Perhaps it helps, too, if those prayers are the loudest, the most fervent and the ones recited most often. If your prayers fail to grab His attention, then perhaps all that gold-leafed ornamentation and shining silverware will catch his eye as the sun glints on it.

The stone you cut from the land also lends permanence. It protects you. Stone can guard the church's treasures against theft. Stone can create walls of silence

Our Norman overlords want the high ground, too. But they're not interested in looking up to the sky. They just want the best vantage point to keep a watch over their underlings. There's safety and there's money to be gleaned in knowing what the snivelling wretches are up to. If they plot against you, then snuff them out as you would a candle. If they fail to work to your satisfaction, have them thrashed. If they buy and sell, then tax them.

Let the church have its share of the spoils and let the church distract the Almighty with all those prayers and entreaties. And while He's thus occupied, you and the Devil can plunder whatever you wish.

Stone is strong. Stone is the best defence against enemies or restless subjects. But, most important of all, stone can't be consumed by fire.

Sunny says all of this.

Osbert, young, eager and earnest, stood before his new master, looking ill at ease. None of the easy charm of his father, Aart.

'Speak,' the Shrike commanded him.

'I have a suggestion, my Lord,' Osbert said. 'I know that stone is to be coveted, that we serfs are only fit to live in houses made of wood, but if we were to replace the burned-down houses with stone buildings two storeys high . . .'

'Why in God's name would a serf need two storeys, boy?'

'Begging your pardon, my Lord. The rent you could raise from such houses could be doubled, and they'll not be consumed by fire or storm, but will stand strong for lifetimes . . .'

'But the cost, boy?'

Osbert handed his master a small piece of vellum. On it, neatly scribed, was a list of the estimated costs and the yield in rental. Should the Shrike wish to glean the money from other sources, here was a list of taxpayers and the income from taxes that might be enforced a little earlier than was normally the case. Osbert had called this a *Community Tax*, where the better-off burghers might be persuaded of the merits of helping those whose homes had been destroyed.

Community spirit? Helping others? The lad was misguided there, but the Shrike's eyes were drawn to the good doctor's generous contribution. That would be a tonic.

'Interesting,' the Shrike purred. 'We raise taxes to build stone houses so that more people might pay rent for more years. Very interesting indeed, young Osbert. You've done well. You're what we call *an asset*. You may proceed with the scheme. Speak to your brother-in-law, Talbot. He'll oversee the erection of these new buildings. An idle good-for-nothing, but a superb mason. Whereas you, young man, are clearly no wastrel but a man of action.'

Osbert made his way back to what, since the recent conflagration, had become their temporary home – the calefactory (normally reserved as the place in which monks might relax together) – in the old part of the cathedral grounds. He was a *somebody* now. Determined that he'd better himself, and break free of the cosy comforts of family, the allure of lazy mediocrity, the safety of anonymity.

But his mother, Edie, wasn't going to let go just yet. She hugged her darling Ossie. His shoulders stiffened. Definitely the withdrawn, the withdrawing type and, as far as Edie was concerned, there was nothing the poor boy could do to change that. He'd always stood a distance from the others. Blessed or cursed with apartness. In summer, the other boys might build mock castles with moistened, sandy soil as they'd started doing since the Norman castles had begun rearing up, and as boys will probably continue doing for as long as castles stand proudly on the horizon. In autumn, the other boys might slip into the cathedral gardens and help themselves to ripe, forbidden fruit, under cover of darkness. In winter, the other lads might don their skates, made of horse bone, strapped to their feet, and go careering off over the ice, uninhibited by fear. In spring, the other boys might share their thoughts about what they'd like to do with the girls. Sometimes, a bolder boy would brag about a boisterous exploit, though, when challenged, he'd crumble. That kiss he claimed he'd planted would prove to be a mere shy glance thrown, the rough-and-tumble only a figment of his imagination.

Osbert had always been mystified by such talk. Why the lies?

Ossie was appalled by the unreliability of the spoken word, Sunny will sigh. He needs the certainty of that which is written and can't be unwritten (because even a crossed out word is still etched indelibly on the vellum). But the spoken word. Stories. They shift more than the wind-driven desert sands. If there *is* truth in there, it's hard to find.

A jewel, lost among a sackful of dross, some might say.

Why doesn't everyone seek the truth? Osbert would fret.

'The trouble with most lads,' Edie would say, stroking her little Ossie's hair and aware that he recoiled slightly, 'is that their lips say what their heads wish for.'

Young Ossie was concerned with his own future betterment, but he needed certainty in the present. Ossie liked predictable outcomes. He found his calling when he discovered two worlds: numbers and the written word. Written words and numbers were like a well-trained cur. Always there for you. Never likely to let you down. Eager and willing to do your bidding.

A well-trained cur can be taught to fetch you something of your choosing. Well-trained numbers are the same. You might ask numbers to apportion themselves into quarters and they will lay themselves before you. Four perfectly-formed and equal parts. You may multiply them, add them together, subtract them and much else besides. They'll neither defy you nor disappoint you. Never mock you.

As for words; they, too, will do as you command, but you must be firm. Without a strong hand they can run amok. You must browbeat them into submission. You must pen them, so that they have no means of escape. Once you've mastered them, they'll serve you well. Written words are tamed words, but the spoken word is not to be trusted. Gossip, mockery, behind-your-back laughter, cruel names: these are all causes for uncertainty and alarm.

It's true, of course, that words written by the wrong hands may try to dazzle or blind you. But don't blame the words.

Blame the scribe. Deep in their hearts, words know that they're there to be guardians of the truth. Lies come and go. The truth endures. If you open a book, even in a dull, badly-lit room, lies will sparkle as brightly as a burst of flame, before they shrivel and die. But the truth will shed an eternal light.

II

Sunny's is a different view of the world to Osbert's. He makes his meagre living conjuring stories from the yonder, weaving unpalatable truths into tasty lies. Bitter reality into something more digestible.

Sunny could charm the bees from their hive with his flowery stories.

'My three loves,' he says. 'My family, my stories and . . .'

He swallows hard as he tastes his grief, even after all these years.

'. . . and Wan.'

Wan. The word that moves him to tears, that wipes the jester's smile from his face.

He takes out his whistle and plays a doleful tune. Then, laying the instrument down, he closes his eyes.

A rare silence reigns while he gathers himself.

He'd held his arms around her, as she'd sat there, after the fire had consumed his home, her prison. She was doing Tway's sobbing as well as her own, because Tway could neither speak nor cry. This was, of course, why the Shrike had chosen Tway.

Mute from birth, prepared for his delectation in a dark room for ten years. So tender she was mouth-watering. The Shrike had impaled her. Brutally and painfully. Tway had borne her pain in silence.

Worth her weight in gold.

Pimp and Nell had gone now. Burned to a crisp in the fiery hell of their own making. The stale who'd lured Tway. And the master who'd enslaved her and then sold her.

Sunny would offer Tway comfort. Love of a sort, though not as deep as his all-consuming love for Wan.

Sunny took Wan by the hand and led her to believe that not all was darkness and badness in this world. They ventured out only at night time in the early days, Wan's eyes still unable to bear the onslaught of daylight. She was like a child, looking at each new thing in fear or wonderment.

'Try to see those ten years in the darkness as a blessing,' Sunny encouraged Wan. 'Shedding light on everything is a joy, but each time the light dawns, our sense of wonderment is diminished a little.'

To acknowledge that we're still in darkness is the key to retaining our sense of wonderment. To admit that we know barely anything is the first step to learning something new. So says Sunny.

He pointed up at the stars, puncturing the dark sky. Too many suns to count. Each of them burning so that they might give the potential for life and light and warmth and comfort.

'The ancients had it right,' he said to her. 'It's the sun and maybe the moon, too, whom we should thank for our lives.'

Wan looked at him blankly.

'Look up and what do you see?' Sunny persisted. 'Each of these pinpricks of light represents something good in the blackness. That star there, shining brightly, is Hope. That one is Friendship. That one is Laughter.'

He continued to pick out stars.

Kindness. Fair-mindedness. Gentleness. Encouragement. Charity. Trust . . .

'What about that?' Wan pointed to the moon.

'Ah, the brightest light in the night sky. The reflected light of the sun, they say. The light to guide you in the darkness. That's Love.'

'What of the sun and the day?' Wan asked.

'The sun? You mustn't look at the sun because it's too bright for our eyes. But the sun is Light and Life itself. Without Light, there can be no Life. Just as without Life there can be no Light. The sun is the Light that eclipses all darkness and death.'

'So if there's so much goodness, then where does badness reside?'

Sunny tapped his forefinger against his right temple.

'Badness resides only in men's heads,' he said. 'Cruelty. Negativity. Mean-spiritedness. Insensitivity. Resentment. And all the rest.'

Wilburh had overheard them. Although touched by Sunny's tenderness, maybe even a trifle moved by his little tale, she couldn't resist a dig at her younger sibling.

'Be careful what you believe, Wan. Sunny's head may not be full of badness, as some men's are, but he makes up for it with hot air and bullshit.'

'Thank you, sister, for your helpful contribution,' Sunny responded.

But Wilburh could see, as every one of them could see, that Sunny and Wan were falling in love. The happy-go-lucky storyteller. And skinny little Wan, with her dark, haunted eyes. Wan, whose strength was growing almost by the moment. Sunny's love was bringing colour to pale Wan's grey, twilit world. Adding love and loveliness to her loveless life.

Tway watched them. Wary of Sunny at first because, although she'd known the little piper since he'd shimmied down into their room and scared them half to death, she was cautious about putting her trust in any man. Pimp and the Shrike had hardly put forward a compelling case for men in general. If the stars in the night sky were symbols of all that's good, then the bruises that marred Tway's moon-white skin were badges of badness. But at least those bruises were slowly, imperceptibly beginning to heal.

Wan and Tway still slept together on one bed. As they'd always done, since being locked together into their room. Two strangers who'd become almost as one. Which presented Sunny – suddenly bashful, for all his storyweaver's bravado – with a problem. Mind you, when you're in love, Sunny says, all challenges seem surmountable.

Sunny and Wan had by now received the Shrike's blessing on their union, though whether a devil can shower you with his blessing is a moot point. Sunny climbed tentatively onto their marital bed. It suddenly seemed a crowded place.

What next? It wasn't easy for Sunny to talk to his father or mother about these matters. Osbert was clueless. Wilburh and Talbot would have to suffice.

'Just follow your instincts. But don't rush,' Wilburh advised.

'Be masterful,' Talbot said. 'In my experience, a woman likes a man who's masterful.'

'How would you know that?' Wilburh scoffed.

'I've had my moments,' Talbot said.

A look of concern flashed across Wilburh's face. What moments? Surely he was jesting. Talbot would never have erred, would he? Then again. What about the times she'd been with child. All those occasions when he'd slipped out for a pint or two of ale. No. Not Talbot. He wasn't the sort.

Talbot didn't even register his wife's concern.

There were three on the bed and the whistle said to Sunny to roll over. And, judging by the sighs and gasps, none of them fell out with one another.

Sunny's marital bed was a crowded but happy place.

There were nudges and winks aplenty: most of them, possibly all of them, administered by Talbot.

'Got your hands full there, Sunny,' he joked.

Wilburh cuffed him.

'Perhaps you should concentrate on planting your seed in me, instead of drooling with envy at Sunny,' she chided him.

'What's the point?' Talbot said, gloomily.

Nine times, he'd planted his seed, he said. Nine times, the Almighty had thought fit to rob them of their child.

'The point is: we should learn never to give up. This time next year I'll be holding a child in my arms. I know it.'

She'd said that before. But Talbot didn't complain. He shrugged his shoulders, pulled down his leggings and got on with it.

What he didn't know was that Wilburh was already well into her pregnancy. But she wasn't going to let on. Why give her shirker of a husband an excuse to forego his carnal duties? Besides, there was a bloom to Tway's cheeks these days. Surely that fact hadn't passed Talbot by. An exhausted husband is a husband less likely to wander. Yes, there was something to be said for keeping a watchful eye on your man. And something to be said in favour of keeping him in the dark, when it came to nighttime fumblings.

As for Sunny and Wan and Tway. Rumours were mongered. Folk gossiped. But it was soon evident that it was Tway, not Wan, whose belly had started to swell.

III

Robin arrived first. Yes, for the one and only time in his life, Robin came first. Without any fuss, either.

As easy as shelling peas, Wilburh says.

Robin's birth was as near to painless as childbirth can be.

'I'll give him three months at best,' Talbot suggested gloomily, when presented with his tenth child.

'For heaven's sake, Talbot,' Wilburh said.

'Hopes are something it's better not to raise,' Talbot said. 'An unraised hope is one that can't be dashed. Dashed hopes are the worst sort of hopes.'

Fortunately, Robin didn't understand a word. He'd cling to his life every bit as tenaciously as his father clings to a point of view.

There was terror in Tway's eyes when, six weeks later, the time came for her child to be delivered.

'Mea culpa,' Sunny said, in a rare excursion into Osbert's beloved Latin. 'And lest anyone should think I'm referring to the deed itself, let me explain. Had I not fed dear Tway with filched capons and other nourishing foods – yes, most of them stolen – then she'd never have built up the reserves to nourish the child growing inside her.'

And nor would she have had to endure what was about to befall her.

She opened her mouth to scream, but only a faint mewing emerged. The child wouldn't come. It was indeed a miracle that the seed had grown within her. Not only Sunny's offerings, but also those hearty stews that Edie and Wilburh had cooked must have done their work.

Right there and then, though, the effort of bringing her baby boy into the world was draining the life tinder from Tway. Tearing her apart.

Wan held her right hand, Edie her left.

'Push,' Edie said, remembering, again, the pain she'd endured. Though remembered pain is never as bad as pain itself.

Tway pushed but nothing would come. She looked into Wan's eyes.

'What was that look telling you?' Edie asked.

'That I should be the mother of her child,' Wan replied.

Edie stroked Tway's hair repeatedly. She could lie to the poor girl and tell her all would be well or she could prepare her to meet her fate.

'Remember to look the Almighty full in the face, Tway,' she said. 'That way he'll see the goodness in your heart. As for your bairn, he or she will have mothers and fathers aplenty in this place.'

When Tway's breathing had finally stopped, they were obliged to cut the child from her.

It was Talbot's chance to be a hero again. The man who – for all his idleness – had a talent for carving stone, held a knife in his left or sinister hand and cut Tway's flesh with a steady arm. The same steady arm that knew how to wield a mallet in order to give shape and life to a pristine block of limestone, with quiet confidence, gentleness, but certainty.

When Eadwerd emerged, bloodied but alive, there was rejoicing and sadness in equal measure. He reached out and grasped Edie's proffered finger with his tiny left hand.

'A cack hander,' Edie smiled. 'Just like your Uncle Talbot.'

Wilburh looked at Talbot and her eyes narrowed, her doubts again came back to haunt her.

No. She banished the thought.

Wan reached down and placed her arms around Tway. Kissed her repeatedly, as if this might somehow bring her back. As she did so, she felt something, someone stirring inside her. An unborn child of her own.

'I'm sorry for your loss, my love,' Sunny said. For once, his whistle remained strapped in his belt. There's a time and a place.

Grief overcame Wan. Fear consumed her. She'd lost Tway. It was as if she'd lost half of herself. For all that Sunny adored her and for all that Tway's baby was there – a flesh-and-bloody reminder of the mother – she felt utterly alone.

What of the bairn inside her? If childbirth had taken Tway's life, would she fare any better? She stood there, pale as a ghost and wailing, while Sunny comforted her.

'Not the best start for the lad,' Talbot said. 'I'll give him three months at best.'

Wilburh struck him a fierce blow across the back of the head. A hero no longer.

IV

To grow up together – as Ed, Robin and I have done – can be comforting or it can be stifling. Eadwerd has to work with Uncle Talbot and Cousin Robin during the day and has to share a home with them at night. Admittedly, we're all spared the discomforts of the one-roomed hovel where Grandfather Aart and Grandmother Edie raised their brood. Whereas Osbert's fled the nest and found some solace in his own quarters, the rest of us are cocooned in a four-roomed, two-storeyed home. We've reaped the benefits of betterment. Talbot points out that we must always spare a thought for those poor souls, worse off than us, who suffer dashed hopes and *worsement*.

When you share so much of your life with another, you tend to grow either shorter-tempered with them or fonder of them. Longer-tempered. Uncle Talbot and Ed are undoubtedly fond of each other. This, despite Uncle Talbot's reputation for oddity and gloominess, and the unnerving way he peers at Ed (and, indeed, everyone else).

'It's all that dust, what with being a stonemason,' he complains. 'It gets in your eyes, so that you can barely see beyond the end of your nose. That and all the smoke when I became a hero that time. Well, that and the fact I may be turning back into a mole again.'

Some call Talbot *unmæge* – iffy. While Ed, Robin and I were growing up and while the other adults bantered around the fire, Talbot sought solace in our company. He'd pick us up, one by one, and peer at us in the gloom.

'The good news is that you'll all be blessed with long lives,' he said. 'The bad news is they'll be full of hardship. Softship is solely the preserve of the Normans. You never hear an Englishman talk about *softship*. As for your moments of happiness, they'll be confined and your joy will be bridled. Do you all know what sort of person benefits from happiness unconfined, and unbridled joy?'

'The Normans,' we chanted.

'Correct. A Norman lives a life of effortless ease and plenty. An Englishman's life is one of effortful, plentiless grind.'

Talbot nodded in the direction of the adults, seated around the fire.

'The trouble with that lot,' he said, 'is that they all look at me in a funny way, as if they think I'm gormless, when in fact I'm actually in possession of lots of gorm.'

'You and I are more alike than you suppose,' Talbot would tell Ed, years later, as they worked together to bring about the betterment of the city of Exeter.

In some respects he's right, Sunny concedes. Talbot's a mason, in charge of many of the building works in the city. He shares in common with Ed the rare gift of being able to carve in a way that could make wood or stone sing. Ed's an apprentice and has lately begun to work with stone, having carved only wood at first. They're also as one in believing Robin to be a dolt, utterly without any talent, who should have his ears boxed at every opportunity. In other words: with Robin, they were both short. With each other, their tempers were long. Where they differ is that while Ed plies his trade with application, Talbot is – as Aunt Wilburh constantly reminds us all – as idle as a fed cat.

'You're beyond hope,' Uncle Talbot rolls his eyes, as Robin unloads another bag of rubble in the wrong place. Hopelessness implies the absence of hope. Robin is able to create the belief that things can only get worse. Perhaps the opposite of hope is despair. Perhaps Robin induces despairfulness.

Uncle Osbert told us that the Almighty had given Eadwerd his dexter hand for a reason and that he should do the Lord's bidding and use it for good. Well he didn't give Ed his right hand for writing. That much I'm sure of. Ed's quill stubbornly refuses to do his, the Lord's, or anyone else's bidding. Though he can use his hands to work a mallet and chisel well enough.

'Our Eadwerd makes love to a block of wood or stone the way some young men might wish to make love to a fair maiden. His carvings blossom or bloom into something beautiful,' Uncle Talbot sighed, only last night. Any talk of lovemaking is now what they call a *sore point*: it had Aunt Wilburh scowling at Talbot.

'Apologies, Perty,' he said.

As for what was said today, I have only Ed's word to go on. But Ed's word is as trusty as the word of God. Uncle Osbert had always said the Almighty gave us all a right hand as part of His plan. Though he was never entirely sure where our left hand fitted in with God's plan.

'Maybe the Almighty should have given us a stump in place of a left hand,' Robin once said, in one of our lessons. Which Uncle Osbert reckoned was possibly the least stupid thing Robin had ever uttered.

Eadwerd finally found out today where his right hand fitted into God's plan. It was for giving Robin a good cuffing. Robin had been taunting Ed about my being fallen and saying they all now called me "Dirty Perty". Ed said to Robin that I'd never once in my life said one word to harm anyone and he had no right to say such things, and that I'd not fornicated. But Robin wouldn't let go.

'Dirty Perty's been taken 'vantage of,' Robin was chanting. Which was when Ed clobbered him.

Uncle Talbot was laughing at Robin.

'Good for you, shutting the blighter up, Ed,' he said.

Robin was prostrate on the floor, his nose was bleeding and Ed had his foot pressed on Robin's chest. He was begging Ed to stop.

'Perty's not even your proper sister,' he was squealing, 'so why should you care?'

'Not proper?' Ed said. 'She's the best sister a brother could ever punch the lights out of another lad for.'

Ed confessed to me that he felt like kicking Robin as he lay there but reckoned you don't go handing out two beatings when one will do. Besides, his right wrist was hurting, which was more of a concern.

'Well if she's a proper sister, then you're damned twice over,' Robin said. 'Once for striking your cousin and once for being in love and all gooey about your sister.'

'I'm not gooey,' Ed told him. 'I love Perty in a brotherly way.'

'I've heard it said from the Bible that it ain't right having thoughts about your sister,' Robin said, being too stupid to stop arguing when his chest was still under Ed's foot.

'Where's it say that?' Ed asked.

'I've seen it clear as day,' Robin said. 'I've seen this verse in some chapter or other. It says: "behold, he that has thoughts that aren't right about his sister and he that strikes a cousin with his right hand, that person shall go to the fiery depths". Except it's in Latin.'

Ed said he knew Robin was lying because he could barely read a word of English, let alone any Latin.

'Besides,' Ed said. 'It's different when you're adopted.'

'You may have been 'dopted by Sunny,' Robin said, 'but that doesn't stop Perty being a true sister if Sunny's a fornicator who put both Wan and Tway in the family way.'

'Just now you were saying Perty's not my proper sister,' Ed said.

'That's as maybe. But think on this. You reap what you sow and if Sunny sowed his seed in Wan and Tway both, then the

Almighty would have punished them to death when you and Perty were born. Which makes you God's punishment and makes Perty your proper sister.'

'You don't know your arse from your elbow,' Ed shouted and he bent down and grabbed hold of Robin again, shaping to strike him, though he wasn't sure which way, on account of his painful wrist.

Talbot decided it was time to intervene.

'Be gone with you, Robin. You'd best shimmy up that scaffolding before *I* clock you, too.'

Robin was off like a rat up a rope.

'Here, let me see that right hand, Ed,' Uncle Talbot said. ''Tis a mercy indeed that you struck the little swine with your right hand and not your left.'

V

Words.

'Sticks and stones may break your bones, whereas words can hurt, but they never harm you,' Sunny said, as he slipped his whistle into his belt and put his arm around me. 'I should know, Perty. It's a jongleur's lot in life to be ridiculed, criticised and generally abused by those who only know how to put a man down, but couldn't conjure a story if their life depended on it.'

I was still sobbing.

'You're hurting inside, Perty,' Sunny said. 'You're hurting because of that pedlar's absence and you're hurting because of Robin's presence. Some pain – especially the pain of loss – is slow to heal. Believe me. I know. There's not a day goes by when I don't think about your mother. But words. They're like chaff in the wind.'

There were three in the bed and the frail one died and in her place, in a Tway-sized space, slept Eadwerd. A constant reminder to Wan of what might lie in store. Wan's sleep was snatched and troubled for worry about the loss of Tway and about the fate that awaited her. So Sunny played his whistle quietly, calling up lullabies because Wan would need all the rest and all the strength she could muster.

'When you finally came, Wan did all the screaming that Tway had never been able to give voice to,' Sunny tells me. 'She screamed her own hurt and she wailed on Tway's behalf, too.'

So much blood and sweat and pain. Why must it be so?

'I'm sorry, my love,' Sunny had said, stroking Wan's damp hair. 'If I'd known what you'd have to endure, I'd have kept my whistle in my leggings.'

'But you were more beautiful than any song I'd ever teased from my whistle, Perty,' Sunny says.

He felt guilt for his thoughtlessness in inflicting pain when he'd only wanted to love Wan. Guilt, but not regret, because if you feel regret or remorse, you'd take the opportunity, if you could, to retrace your steps and then set out in a different direction.

'Looking into the eyes of my lovely newborn daughter, holding her in his arms, it was impossible to unwant you, Perty,' Sunny says, 'because my love for you overwhelmed any other emotion.'

Unbeknown to Sunny, as I breathed new life into my lungs, my mother Wan was dying. Sunny might not have known it, but Wan did. She'd try to hang onto life for as long as she could, but – like someone clutching a cliff face – you can only hold out for so long.

Wan's strength had been sapped by her ordeal. Slowly, day by day, her resolve drained from her. Hour by hour, the darkness that had surrounded her while she'd been incarcerated by Pimp – but that had, too fleetingly, been banished from her life – inched forward, readying itself to snatch her back. To reclaim her. The sky watched her, gloomily. Its countenance darkened. The clouds wept. The stars lost their sparkle. The moon dimmed. And finally, a fortnight after the birth of her daughter, Wan's sun went out. So says Sunny.

And now, he looks into my eyes and he swears I'm the very image of my late mother.

'You, my darling, have been showered with all the blessings denied my beloved Wan. It's a girl's lot, in this, the year of our Lord Eleven Hundred and Thirty-Five, to become one of only three things: a wife, a nun or a whore. In each case a life of obedience. To a husband, to God or to a Pimp. Your grandmother, Edie, narrowly escaped becoming a nun. Your mother narrowly avoided becoming a whore. And you, my dear Perty, because you have the bright mind and spiritedness of Edie and Wan, have narrowly averted the tragedy of becoming Ossie's wife. You are indeed blessed.'

Words. They always came tumbling out by the mouthful, where Sunny was concerned.

VI

Eadwerd was still in pain on account of having given Robin a cuffing. And so I wrapped his wrist in clean rags.

'You've inflicted a sprain on yourself, Ed,' I told him.

'You and I must stop getting ourselves in scrapes,' he said.

'I'm grateful to you,' I told him. I was at a low ebb. No girl wants to be talked about as if they're unclean.

'It's as our father said,' he added. 'I'd never forsake you, Perty. If you descended to the very depths of despair, I'd be beside you and I'd take your hand and lead you into the light.'

I started weeping again. I don't know why. Relief or sadness.

Robin came up to me, looking sheepish.

'Father says I must 'pologise, so I'm sorry, Perty, for what they call honouring your impunity.'

'You got that arse about face,' Ed said. 'You impugned Perty's honour.'

'Well I've 'pologised, so you can't go crying over spilt milk,' he said.

Which is a daft thing to say, even by Robin's standards, for there are plenty of people who'd weep for the loss of a pitcher of milk.

In truth, Ed wasn't angered so much by Robin as he was – still is – by Bernard, whom he still calls "that fox" or "that snake-in-the-grass pedlar". I want to tell Ed I still have feelings for Bernard, but I daren't.

Today, after I'd completed my chores, I made my way back to the house to prepare a rare treat alongside Grandmother Edie.

She could see my heart was elsewhere. Bernard might just as well have taken it from me and carried it off in his bag the way he does those relics.

'The heart-shaped hole's the deepest hole that can be cut from us,' Grandmother Edie said. 'All that love we had to give and it's snatched away. And the only thing that can fill the void is more of the same. Love. From your kith and kin.'

'You never lost Grandfather Aart, though.'

'Oh but I did. I thought he'd been taken from me. I was a novice nun. I was in love with him. So much so I thought I was going to swoon with joy when he kissed me. But the abbess thought such behaviour unbecoming and locked me away from him. I ached for him, Perty.'

'But you got him back.'

'Yes. I got Aart back. And you'll get Love back, but whether that's Bernard or another man, I can't say.'

Time to prepare the eels, she said.

You must first soak them in cold water. Then rinse them well. You should slit the skin below the gills, pin their heads hard against a nail so that they hang and then you can peel back the skin. Then you chop off their heads and watch while they wriggle, as if between life and death, still dreaming of slithering through glorious, thick mud, as they embark on their afterlife.

Then you must grill them over the fire and watch the fat drip from them before you add them to the stew.

'Why did the Almighty make something so tasty such a challenge to prepare?' I asked.

'Maybe the Almighty wanted us to learn that the best things – like love and eels – don't come easily but they're worth all the effort,' Grandmother Edie suggested.

The eel stew was all the tastier for being the first fish or meat to have touched our lips for some weeks. It must have stirred something in Uncle Talbot because, for once, he wasn't clouded by an air of gloom. First he praised the stew and then he praised Ed.

'You son has gifts,' he told Sunny. He ruffled Ed's hair (which Ed wasn't best pleased about, given that Talbot's hands stank of eel, though Ed didn't complain). 'I'm proud that he should be my 'prentice, for I'll be able to bask in what they call the *reflected glory*. Furthermore, his right hand is as useful as his left and is good at silencing little coxcombs that prance on the scaffolding. A mason in the making, Ed. Just like your talented uncle.'

Wilburh rolled her eyes. He was a good-for-nothing, was Talbot.

VII

I'd done my duties, fed all the animals. Ed found me outside the main city gate, watching the road to Lyme. I don't mind admitting that my heart leaped each time I saw a speck on the horizon.

'It grieves me to see your pain, Perty,' Ed said, settling down beside me, 'though I think you should try to banish him from your mind.'

It's true, I know. My father's whistle has declared it so. That Bernard loved me only with his lips and the honeyed words that tumbled from them. Which is just as paltry a form of love as Uncle Osbert's. My uncle knows many things. What use is it, though, to understand Latin but not to comprehend the beauty in a violet, not to feast on its loveliness the way a bee might become drunk on its nectar?

I told Ed this was so. I also acknowledged that, whereas Uncle Osbert's behaviour can be exasperating, Bernard's actions were despicable. I admitted that reason says I should despise Bernard, but reason walked out of the door the moment he looked into my eyes.

'There are still those who love you with all their heart, Perty,' he said. 'I've watched how Grandfather Aart and Grandmother Edie cherish you. Father, too. Despite all his prattle about his whistle that I'd sometimes gladly snap into two pieces for all its insolence and smugness, father loves you so much he'd lay down his life for you. Me too, Perty. No brother could wish for a finer sister than you.'

I wept at that.

It seems to me that Ed always has me either weeping or laughing.

Ed tells me that Robin's been as annoying as a midge that won't let you be, these last few days. Nor has Robin forgiven Ed for the beating he handed out.

'I think you wounded his pride more than his numskull's head,' I said.

'Last week, Robin was all for saying Sunny was a fornicator and lay with Wan and Tway, both. Now he says that Talbot's hands are all over me and he's forever stroking my hair and telling me I have special gifts. He reckons Talbot has a mind to fornicate with me.'

'It seems to me that Robin's very vexed over the matter of fornication. Perhaps on account of the fact he'd like to do some fornicating of his own but can't find a girl daft enough or desperate enough to agree.'

'Not even that mermaid,' Ed said. 'And I doubt she has many proposals of marriage.'

We were giggling now.

'Tell me, Perty,' Ed asked, of a sudden. 'Does my hair smell of eel stew?'

'No more than usual,' I said, after I'd sniffed it.

'That's all right then,' he laughed.

VIII

Sunny's playing a lively melody on his whistle. Perhaps by playing the tune of our past so loudly, he's drowning out those inner voices that haunt me.

On with the story, he says.

Osbert had done well. He was planning his betterment with all the precision he deployed in the rebuilding of the Shrike's coffers and his new empire, wrought in stone.

Indeed. No stone was left unturned. The boy who'd spent his early years looking anxiously towards the dark corners of their one-roomed hovel, watching out for boggarts, had become a man who checked in the dark recesses of the ledger for the tiniest miscalculation. Pored over his fellow clerks' workings, unearthing even the smallest inaccuracy. Depending on your perspective, Osbert was either a godsend or a pain in the arse. Most – including the Shrike's and his family's clerks – thought the latter. The Shrike most definitely thought the former, and his was the one opinion that mattered.

Buildings went up, Osbert's standing increased. The rents came in, the Shrike's coffers swelled. The plan was working.

'We must not allow ourselves to wallow,' Osbert had chided Sunny, demonstrating his utter lack of sensitivity as Sunny continued to mourn the absence of his beloved Wan. 'Loss is not something we should grieve over. We must embrace it as an opportunity for betterment. A house burned to the ground is not a timber-framed house destroyed. It is the opportunity for a stone edifice to be raised. Witness the gleaming two-storeyed homes now being built. Compare them to what went before. Permanence must replace impermanence. Iron-willed determination must replace maudlin reflection.'

Sunny had ignored Ossie's advice. Just as he'd always done. He'd picked up his whistle, turned his face away and played a plaintive love song.

'Oh, by the way,' Osbert had announced to the family. 'Thanks to my efforts, new quarters will be available for the family in a matter of weeks. Although some of you might be undeserving,' – he threw a contemptuous look at Sunny – 'I feel a sense of duty to my family. The master has graciously agreed that the first rooms to be completed should be made available to my kin.'

Edie had got up, walked over and kissed Ossie on the forehead.

'Thank you, Ossie,' she'd said. 'You're a fine and feckful young man.'

Osbert had borne the compliment – and indeed his mother's kiss – with an air of resigned forbearance.

Sunny's whistle says that if you've no heart, your heart can never be broken. His was broken when Wan died. Smashed into a thousand fragments. But it's slowly been put back together, piece by piece. Built, one day at a time, by the kind deeds of others, by friendship and family. Mended, smile upon smile, by increments of laughter and love.

He turns to me.

'You, Perty, are possessed of your grandmother's joy. You have your late mother's quiet grace. And – though I say it myself – you also have your father's pluckiness.'

Of course he'd been grateful to Osbert for his efforts on all their behalves, but he'd opt for love over betterment or riding-roughshod-over-others, any day of the week.

IX

Ed, Robin and I were playing at sword, vellum, stone. It's a game as old as the most ancient of the trees growing on the Devonshire hills that surround our city. It's a game that Wilburh, Osbert and Sunny played when they were young. On the count of three you take your hands from behind your back and present a pointed finger, a flat palm or a clenched fist.

It's the one game that Robin can play on an even footing because it's entirely down to chance. No skill or intellect is called for.

Sunny insists that it's a game that reflects life, for there are three ways to exert power over others. The power of the wielded sword, the power of the spoken or written word and the power derived from stone fortresses. All of them more potent and less potent than the others. If a sword is run through a man who speaks persuasively, he's no longer able to exercise his power. So the sword is mightier than the pen. A stone castle can't be breached even by a vast army of men striking their swords impotently against the walls. Stone is mightier than the sword. And yet, while buildings are raised and then they fall, the word – language and truth - is eternal. Etched vellum is mightier than stone.

Osbert entered the room. Vexed, though not by the game. He'd always felt – as Robin now feels – that it was a game where he wasn't disadvantaged when faced with Wilburh's fleetness or Sunny's guile.

Osbert had always looked on stiffly as his older sister, Wilburh, and his younger brother, Sunny, little more than a toddler, had clambered over walls or thrown each other a bound-up ball of cloth to catch. He'd envied their easy grace, the way they could duck and dive and weave as deftly as rodents when they joined in a communal game of tag. Osbert always stood a distance from them, seeming for all the world to be judging them. That look of studied indifference.

'Catch,' Wilburh had laughed whenever she'd tossed Ossie the ball of rags. Ossie would flap at it, like someone trying to grapple with an eel.

The other kids would laugh as Osbert slunk off to seek comfort in books and the written word, to find solace in quiet contemplation.

Bettering himself.

Uncle Osbert says something gracious. Courageous, even.

'I believe,' he says, swallowing hard, 'that you were right to decline my proposal of marriage, Perty. It's fitting that you should have spurned my advances. I also believe you would be right-minded to forget that pedlar. He's as unworthy of you as I am. You are utterly without guile and motivated only by love. This is a gift to be cherished.'

I stood on my toes, flung my arms around his neck and kissed him.

'Thank you, Uncle Osbert,' I said.

He broke into an embarrassed smile. I wondered if the absence of Dog, and Dog's undying devotion, has moved him. Wondered if he's finally learned that there's more to life than mere betterment.

X

I was looking out to the horizon again, watching the Lyme road. Every day, hope drains a little from you, but it never quite dies. Like the bluebells or the wild garlic in the woods whose leaves have all browned and then been spirited away, but they rise again with the spring warmth and are in flower once more, come May. Hope was only sleeping. It hadn't died.

Then I saw a speck appear. It walked towards me. I could see this was no man, but I wondered at first what animal it might be. It walked with purpose, though not with confidence. It was only when he was nearer that I knew for sure. Uncle Osbert's cur, Dog. He came up to me, his tail wagging, but not with the usual vigour. I could have wept because he was such a forlorn sight. He looked half-starved and gave every appearance of having been sorely birched. He was happy to see me and I him. Dog and I forgot our woes for a moment as I took him in my arms. He was as light as a hen. In truth, I think I was glad it was Dog and not Bernard who'd returned. A cur cares not one jot whether you're fallen, you've stumbled or you're still an unsullied maiden. A cur loves you as he finds you, with every fibre of his being. A cur's first thought is to love any man or woman wholeheartedly, unless he's given reason to feel otherwise. People could learn much from curs. No one, nothing is more giving and forgiving than a cur. Not even the blessed Redeemer. Perhaps if the Almighty had Himself been a cur, then ours would have been a world without malice or selfishness or deceit, but a world of love and loyalty and forgiveness.

I carried Dog through the city gates and found him some cool water, to ease his panting. Then I took him to our home to await the arrival of Osbert on his regular evening visit.

And when my uncle walked through the door, it was the nearest I'd ever seen him to being overcome by emotion, until he pulled himself together and put on his usual air of indifference.

'The cur has gained ingress into our home and into our affections,' he admitted, reluctantly. 'I've no fatted calf to prepare for the prodigal, but tomorrow I shall procure a large bone and present it to my charge,' he announced.

Robin spoke up.

'Don't seem right to me,' he said. 'All day, I've seen women of various shapes and sizes holding Dog to their bosoms. I reckon I could do worse than run off and get soundly birched by a bunch of scoundrels so that some maiden might hold me to her bosom.'

'There are easier ways to woo a maid, lad,' Talbot said, 'though being a degree less wholesome than a cur, you might have to venture further afield than Dog, to earn your reward.'

XI

Eadwerd found me all alone and seated in my favourite meadow. We've always come here together, since we were not much higher than the summertime grass. We'd lie down and not make a sound, hiding while Robin sought us. We'd play a game we called *adder's bite* where you must grab the foot of those who try to find you, before they see you. It wasn't much of a game, because the adder always lost, but that didn't stop our being coiled to springing with excitement each time we lay in wait. Perhaps therein lies a lesson in life. The anticipation of many things is more enjoyable than the things themselves.

When we were young, I'd name every flower and every butterfly in the meadows, for which credit must go to my father, Sunny.

'Wan and Tway never once saw a butterfly or a flower when they were growing, after their imprisonment,' he said. 'You must never take any living thing for granted, Perty, but must be thankful each day for sunlight and the gift of beauty it bestows.'

'He's never coming back, Perty,' Ed told me, as he sat beside me, and though I knew in my heart that it was true and I also knew it was for the best, it nevertheless cut me to the quick.

I began sobbing.

'You should face up to it, Perty,' he persisted. 'It was in all likelihood him that birched Dog and he'd have treated you badly, too.'

He shaped to put his arm around me and I pushed him away, then rose to my feet.

'Do you enjoy being so cruel?' I snapped at him.

I walked away. From Ed and from the truth.

'Sorry, Perty,' I heard him shout after me.

I still felt hurt when I came back to the house later. That was when Aunt Wilburh sat me down.

'Ed did aright, Perty,' she said. 'Sometimes we turn our heads, because it's hard to stare the truth full in the face. We need those who love us to point the way. Some brave soul had to tell you the truth and it was best coming from him who loves you most.'

'Should I apologise to Ed?' I asked.

'In my experience, it's best not to go around apologising to men. They already believe they're right on most things, without being given the least encouragement, but I think Ed may be different to the likes of Talbot, whose skin is as thick as the bark of a tree.'

Uncle Osbert was seated on a stool, chuntering.

'What's vexes you, Ossie?' Aunt Wilburh asked. 'Does my talk of the failings of men distress you?'

'Forgive me,' Osbert replied. 'I wasn't listening to a word. Of greater concern is the fact that these shoes have blistered my feet.'

'Serves you right for buying new ones, Ossie. You can soften leather up by steeping it in dog shit, as I'm sure you know. Perhaps Dog will oblige,' Wilburh teased him.

'As ever, I have absolutely no intention of following your advice, sister,' he said.

'Well, on your feet be it, Ossie,' Wilburh sighed.

'I've nothing against excrement per se,' Osbert said. 'Indeed, like any man of good station I hang my finery in my garderobe where the stench of stool keeps the moths at bay, but I draw a line at smearing canine crap on my leather shoes.'

'When a man would rather hobble around in pain than go about his business smelling like a tannery, we call this *vanity*,' Sunny observed.

'I call it *having basic standards of cleanliness*,' Osbert responded.

XII

There was much excitement today when the late Seigneur's first-born – elder brother of the Shrike – came by to inspect the work Uncle Talbot was leading.

Talbot introduced Ed, claiming he was the finest apprentice he'd ever had under his command. His Lordship spoke to Ed, informing him of his envy for he, too, would have wished to have been a carver, had it not been his lot in life to attend to matters of state and suchlike.

Uncle Osbert – Overseer of the Works – was standing there, stiffly.

'You've turned out a fine young man,' the Shrike's elder brother said. Or rather Osbert said, interpreting his master's words.

'Thank you, Uncle Osbert,' Ed replied.

'Don't thank me. Thank your master.'

'Thank you, my Lord.'

At which point, the new Seigneur slipped a penny into Ed's hand.

Robin was in the darkest of moods, consumed with envy, given that their lord and master had showed no interest in the block of stone he was carrying at the time.

'Building work may cease,' his Lordship announced.

Then he was off, with Osbert, limping pitifully behind him and wincing with every tread, on account of his new shoes.

It's the time for haymaking and those of us who are fit enough must join together to cut and gather the hay. There's no money for such work: only pride and some provisions, a pitcher of ale and much singing and merriment, but we know to play our part, for if there's no haymaking or harvest then we'll all starve.

Ed's strong enough – with his apprentice stonemason's shoulders – to stand beside Talbot now and lift the hay into the carts. Robin, too, though he shows signs of being a shirker to add to the fact of his having a wagging, gossip's tongue that reports back to me conversations that should have remained private. It's true enough that to be in possession of gossip is a fine thing, but gossip is like proximity. It can be a comfort and it can bind a group of souls together, but it can tear the same group apart and destroy it as quickly as any contagion, too.

'You and I are kinsmen, Ed,' Talbot said to Eadwerd. 'You can speak the truth. When I look into your eyes, I see a lad deep-smitten in love and a lad racked by worries.'

'Tell me honestly, Uncle Talbot. Are Perty and I true brother and sister? I've heard gossip from certain quarters that my father fornicated with both Wan and Tway.'

'I can assure you, Ed. Sunny is no fornicator. His one love was Wan. She was like a tiny bird, trapped in a dark place and Sunny's love gave her wings. We don't decide whom or when we can love. Love calls out to us. Sunny protected Tway. Loved her as a sister, but not as a wife. But if you fear otherwise, know this: Sunny loves you and Perty in equal measure. He'd lay down his life for either of you.'

'Then who *is* my father?' Ed asked.

'Please don't press me, Ed,' Talbot replied. 'Let it suffice to know that you're loved as a son and a brother.'

But that had Ed vexed even more, for it finally dawned on him, as it had dawned on Wilburh long before – though she narrowed her eyes and kept her counsel – that Talbot might be Ed's father. Which would explain all those times he'd placed his arms around Ed and told him how proud he was. It might explain, also, why they were both carvers who could make stone sing with its beauty and why they should both prefer to use their sinister hands and not their right, or dexter hands.

Then again. Isn't there another obvious explanation. The Shrike. Was it not he who lay there, drunk, beside Tway when the flames of hell descended and consumed Pimp and Nell? The Shrike must be the father. And yet. It's widely known among the citizens of Exeter, isn't it? That the Shrike's impaled many a maiden, but, in all that time, not once has he managed to sow his seed. It's the judgement of the Almighty, perhaps: punishing the Shrike for being in league with the Devil. The Shrike can't be the father, can he?

What's the truth? Some might say it was Sunny who fathered Ed, some might claim it's the Shrike and some might think it was Talbot. The truth is that he's loved as a son. Isn't this the only truth that matters?

XIII

I felt restless. For once, having eaten my pottage, I wished to be away from our crowded home.

'I'm going for a walk,' I announced.

'An excellent idea,' Osbert said, standing up. 'I, too, am unable to bear the very idea of your father's shrill piping and mindless prattle. Allow me to accompany you, Perty. It's unwise for a young woman to walk the vile streets of Exeter at night.'

'Well, don't go pestering my precious daughter with any further propositions,' Sunny quipped.

Osbert reddened.

'For God's sake,' he said.

'Enough, Sunny,' Edie said. 'It's very gracious of Ossie to look out for his brother's daughter.'

'I hadn't meant to impose myself . . .' Osbert began.

'Thank you, Uncle Osbert,' I said. 'That would be kind.' I couldn't have borne his look of hurt, had I declined him.

It was a warm night and brightly moonlit. Osbert walked beside me, his hands clasped behind his back. Dog, over whom my uncle seemed to be gaining some dominion, walked beside us, occasionally being diverted by some stench or other, before Osbert summoned him. Dog. The one word sufficed. Curs are quick to understand these things.

He apologised to me again.

'I'd merely assumed that you wished to have some time alone and, with my being more comfortable with silence and contemplation than my brother, thought you might welcome my presence.'

'I'm very grateful to you, Uncle Osbert,' I said.

He was wincing less than he had been, as we walked. I observed that he had his worn old shoes back on his feet.

'Sometimes we can glean comfort from that which is most familiar,' he said. 'Sometimes betterment – particularly in the matter of shoes – requires too much in the way of pain for a man to bear.'

'Indeed,' I said. 'Sometimes things are best if we accept them as they are.'

'You have a wise head on those maiden's young shoulders, Perty,' he said. 'Furthermore, I must confess that I've missed your presence at our tutorials, though the same can't be said for your cousin or brother. To teach an able pupil is a joy. To be confronted by stupidity such as Robin's is too much to bear. As for Eadwerd, I believe that his skills lie in the matter of stonemasonry, rather than scribing.'

'I've missed the lessons, too,' I said. He smiled, wistfully.

We walked on in silence for a while.

'When the time comes for you to embrace change, which may be sooner than you know, then you'll be a most excellent wife for some fortunate man. I trust that he'll value you for the jewel you are.'

'Thank you, Uncle Osbert,' I said. 'I never meant to hurt you, when I declined your generous offer.'

'I don't believe you're capable of an unpleasant thought or mean-spiritedness of any kind, Perty,' he said.

There was silence again for a while, broken by the occasional word of greeting from a passer-by, or a rebuke from Osbert, either to Dog or some reprobate or other, slumped in the gutter.

We'd reached his quarters. He offered to walk me the short journey back home again, but I declined.

'Thank you, Uncle Ossie,' I said and, stepping onto the tips of my toes, I kissed my dear, starchy old uncle on his cheek.

'Goodbye then,' he said.

As he shaped to close the door on the world, he saw Dog sitting there, a look of undiminished awe and love written on the cur's face.

In a moment of weakness, he signalled to Dog that he might enter. Dog was beside himself with joy. Ossie sighed. Yes, a cur's love and loyalty can make this hostile world seem a mite more tolerable. Ossie took Dog's head in his hands and ruffled his coat.

Dog could have died of happiness.

XIV

'We're not brother and sister, Perty,' Ed told me, as we made our way to work in the morning. 'I have it on good authority from Uncle Talbot, though I need to delve deeper. I fear Talbot, himself, may be my father and I'm at a loss as to what I should do.'

'Will Sunny talk?' I asked.

'He says Uncle Talbot's the only man who can spill the truth. He reckons even his blessed whistle refuses to tell him the facts. He also says he has no wish to know whom the father might be. So long as he lives in ignorance of this, he can love me as his own son,' Ed told me.

'Strong drink will loosen his tongue,' I suggested.

Strong drink is masterful at drawing out all sorts of things: kept secrets, pent-up anger, unexpressed longing. There's always a price to pay. Strong drink exacts its toll. In changed lives and thumping headaches.

'We'll have to get Uncle Talbot as drunk as a thane.'

And so it was that, as Uncle Talbot sat there, his leggings removed, tracing the lines of his swollen veins and telling us stories of how he'd tunnelled his way out of this scrape or that one, Ed and I plied him with ale.

We were all gathered in our home. The whole family, including Osbert and Dog. The adults had been talking together, unconcerned by our prattling, though Aunt Wilburh had thrown the occasional wary glance Talbot's way.

That was when Ed asked him straight.

'I must know this, Uncle Talbot. You're my father, are you not?'

He guffawed. Then he hauled himself to his feet. He raised his tankard and motioned towards Grandfather Aart.

'You, my dear father-in-law, have always espoused the truth. The truth is like a cur.'

He raised his tankard again, this time towards Dog, who looked up, expectantly.

'The truth, like a cur, is a good friend who serves you well, though sometimes it comes back to bite you. It's time the truth be told. I shall probably be cursed for saying it, cursed for not saying it, but Ed and I are more flesh and blood than any of you might suppose.'

He had them gripped, now. Sunny even laid down his whistle.

'First things first,' Talbot continued. 'A story needs a beginning. Until this moment, I've jealously guarded the secret of my genesis. With very good reason. While the late Seigneur still lived, I might have lost my tongue for saying what I'm about to reveal.'

He paused. We waited in rapt silence.

'My secret,' he then told us, 'is that I am the fruit of the late Seigneur's loins, for he was a fornicator, but a fornicator with a heart, given that, having raped my mother in a moment of need, he at least pledged to provide for me, when she threw herself at his mercy, some months later. She was of a weak disposition and I believe she forsook food and nourishment so that I might survive. I never knew her, but I was placed in the hands of an upstanding couple. Though, when I say upstanding, my new father had one leg and was prone to falling over and my new mother was doubled up with arthritis. Before what must have been my tenth year, my upstanding, stand-in carers had keeled over. Which is understandable, given their ages at the time, which seemed extensive.'

Talbot was rambling. Nevertheless his audience remained riveted.

'See here,' he said, pointing to his right leg. 'My past is mapped out by these swollen veins of mine. That scattering of small purple channels: that's the trauma of my early years. It maps the death of my mother. Where these two veins come to an end: that's . . .'

'In the name of the Redeemer, will you please get on with the story,' Osbert snapped.

'Easy, Ossie. You've a temper shorter than a Norman's. Excitable bunch. We Saxons have what our masters call *sang froid* running through our veins.'

'I thought you said your father was a Norman,' Aunt Wilburh challenged Talbot.

'For God's sake don't hold him up,' Osbert barked. That set Dog off.

'Anyway, the Seigneur continued to watch over me, with an occasional word or two in the right ears. I think they call it *nepotism*, though, being Overseer of the Works and a Norman arse-licker, Ossie will be able to confirm this or otherwise . . .'

Osbert scowled. Dog growled.

'. . . and I was made a 'prentice carver and I found at last that I was possessed of a gift.'

'Certainly no gift for brevity,' Sunny said. Talbot ignored him.

'Then, I met Wilburh and moved in with you, my beloved family. Dear, dear father-in-law Aart. And dear, dear mother-in-law Edie. And dear, dear . . .'

'Oh for Christ's sake, get on with it,' Osbert instructed him.

'Indeed, Ossie. Moving forwards at a canter to that time when I, Talbot, was in the prime of my life, when the conflagration consumed our former home. Who was it, you will recall, who, having been in a former life a mole, was able to burrow through the smoke and help to retrieve first Tway and then the Shrike? It was of course me, and I am able to confirm that the man who had lain, drunk, beside Tway before the flames of hell descended upon her was the Seigneur's second-born son. The Shrike had indeed impaled Tway and beaten her frail body so that it would turn black and blue. But I can also confirm that he isn't the father of the child Tway bore. Which is to say Eadwerd. The Shrike, as is widely known, is incapable of siring any offspring.'

'You're drunk, Talbot. You're rambling and we seem to be no nearer the truth than when you embarked on this endless confession,' Wilburh said.

'Drunk. There's the clue. Let me tell you the truth. I know the truth because the man who deflowered Tway charged me with keeping a watchful eye over Eadwerd. The night before the Shrike arrived, demanding that he be served up with one or other of Pimp's prized virgins, the Shrike's own father, the Seigneur, had paid Pimp well for the same privilege. Pimp, being among the shrewdest of businessmen, and seeing that the Shrike was too blind drunk to know any different, had offered up Tway again, knowing that he would still then be in possession of one prized virgin rather than none. I know this because the late Seigneur, God rest his soul, informed me that I must keep an eye on my half-brother. For, as I've said, he was a fornicator, but one with a heart. Upon my miserable, gloomy life, it's the late Seigneur who was Eadwerd's father. I was subsequently sworn – on pain of death – to tell no man of this. And since that time, the late Seigneur and then his firstborn son (who, like me, was drawn into the secret, though not until his father lay dying) kept their eyes on Eadwerd, here.'

'Well, well,' Grandfather Aart said.

'I think you could perhaps put your leggings back on now, Talbot,' Grandmother Edie suggested.

'Why tell us all this?' Aunt Wilburh asked. 'Why not tell us all this years ago? On the other hand, why risk everything by telling us now?'

'Because . . .' Talbot hesitated. 'Because. You see these two veins here?' He stopped short, shook his head. 'No. I cannot say it, because, knowing my luck, I'll spoil things. The future will curdle in my hands if I go stirring things up. Everything I touch – excepting blocks of stone – is spoiled . . .'

'What Talbot cannot say is that Fate has decreed that he must spill the story now. Fate and an excess of strong ale,' Sunny said, picking up his whistle. 'Without the truth there can be no love. The truth has set love free. So says the whistle.'

XV

Talbot could look none of us in the eye when he awoke in the morning, his head as sore as a bee sting.

'I've shamed myself,' he muttered.

'You've spent a lifetime shaming yourself,' Aunt Wilburh told him.

'Possibly so. But now I've burdened you all with my secrets,' he said.

'Not a burden,' Sunny said. 'A release.'

I, for one, was glad to know the truth. I spoke to Ed when we were alone.

'I hope that you'll still love me, Perty,' Ed said. 'Even though I'm the late Seigneur's son.'

He looked so forlorn that I kissed him on the cheek.

'You could be the spawn of the very devil himself, Ed,' I said to him, 'but you'd still be my brother and my best friend, whom I couldn't ever stop loving.'

We sat together for a while, as Ed waited for the other apprentices to arrive. We listened to the singing of the birds. I told him the different songs. I pointed out how some of them are as regular and predictable as Uncle Osbert and how some – like a throstle – are all free-flowing and as rambling as one of Uncle Talbot's tales. I told Ed that sometimes the truth comes sweeping through the room, as it had done with Uncle Talbot's revelation. How it makes you see the world anew. Then I confessed that I was pleased Ed had hurt me by telling me Bernard wouldn't ever return, for that was another truth worth telling.

'It's called *clearing the air*, Perty,' Ed said.

Just as the sunlight slowly parts the morning mists, so the truth causes us to see everything with greater clarity.

'The truth is you're dearer than a brother, Ed,' I said.

He put his left arm over my shoulder.

'And the truth is you'll always be dearer than a sister, Perty he said. 'The Almighty gave me this arm to wrap you in my brotherly love, just as he gave me my left hand to wield a mallet and my right hand to give a good cuffing to vexatious gossip-mongers such as Robin.'

XVI

When he arrived home, after another evening playing his pipe and telling his jongleur's tales, Sunny had clearly had an egg flung at him.

Two of them, by the look of it. His hair was streaked by the glossy gloop and the yellow yolks.

He ran his right forefinger through his hair and then licked it.

'At least they were fresh,' he said. 'If you're going to be pelted with eggs, it's preferable that they're not rotten ones. The best ones are hard-boiled ones with their shells removed, but I've never yet been hit by one of those.'

He'd apparently had a heated exchange with one of his audience. He'd told them the story of the Merchant of Honiton. You possibly know it. The merchant dreams three times that if he treks to London Bridge, he'll find a fortune. (In such tales, most things come in threes). But after three days and three nights, he's lost his faith in the power of dreams.

'Why so despondent?' a passer-by asks him.

'I've lost my faith in the power of dreams,' the merchant says.

'Never do that,' the passer-by says. 'Only last night, I dreamed of a crock of gold beneath the apple tree in the garden of some idiot merchant from Honiton. If I had the faintest idea where Honiton was, I'd be on my way there already.'

With that, the merchant makes his way back home and, after digging beneath his apple tree, his dreams – all three of them – come true.

'Nonsense. You're talking crap,' a heckler shouted out.

'Stand up and say that,' Sunny challenged the disembodied voice.

The man stood up as bidden. He was a good eighteen inches taller than Sunny and twice as wide at the shoulders.

Bravado is no bad thing in a storyteller, but an excess of it can land you in some difficulty.

'It weren't Honiton. It were Crediton,' the heckler said, angrily. Then, he pitched two eggs in quick succession towards Sunny's head. Pitched them, in fact, with great accuracy. And pitched them with considerable force.

'That's for giving Honiton the glory for what's rightly Crediton's,' the man shouted. 'It were the pedlar of Crediton what were the idiot.'

'Thus proving,' Sunny now says as he stands in front of his family, his hair coated in egg, 'that every pitcher tells a story.'

'And also proving,' Talbot adds, 'that sooner or later, most storytellers end up with egg on their faces.'

'I reckon the days of bards standing up and telling their tales are numbered, Sunny,' Wilburh adds.

'How else are we going to pass on our stories?' Sunny scoffs.

'Scribe them?'

'There's no money to made from scribing fanciful stories, sister.'

XVII

It's the longest day of the year. It's Eleven Hundred and Thirty-Five and it's the most precious day of my life.

Eadwerd and I were walking past the uncut summer meadow, and we saw all the greens and yellows and whites of the grass and flowers. Then a show of orchids – bright purple – caught our eyes, for they stood out, all beautiful and delicate and precious as those jewels that are beyond the means of most English girls.

'You're my orchid, Perty,' Ed said. 'Rare and lovely and you stand out from the rest.'

I was willing him to kiss me, because there was longing in his eyes.

'Thank you,' I said and held his hand, instead. His left hand. Because his right was still bandaged.

Then I jokingly called him *my Lordship* on account of his parentage and said that one day he might own the very fields in which we stood, though I hoped he'd not turn out to be a fornicator like his father, the late Seigneur.

We laughed. Then he drew breath.

'You know that I love you and Sunny, even though you're not my true sister and father?' he asked.

'Of course,' I said.

'And you know every flutter of my heartbeat and everything that causes me anguish and everything that brings me joy?'

'Of course,' I said.

'Then you know that I love you more than a brother should love a sister,' he said.

'Of course,' I said.

Then he turned and – showing spirit – kissed me full on my lips. I was as forward as Aunt Wilburh had ever been in the matter of courtship and welcomed his embrace.

Sunny's whistle had been right. It always is. There are those who'd love you only with their heads, those who'd love you only with their lips and those who'd love you with their hearts.

When a lad kisses you in a heartfelt way, then you'll know.

It was Grandmother Edie and not the whistle who'd told me that.

'You're the best friend I could dream of,' he said, after a while that I'd wished could last for ever. 'I love you as much as life itself, Perty. I should like to declare my love for you to the whole wide world.'

'Perhaps it might be best if we just whisper our secret to Sunny, first,' I said.

But tonight, it being Midsummer Eve, we'll dance, Eadwerd and I. I shall have eyes only for him and he for me. For I know the truth, now. That he is my love and always has been and always will be, for as long as I have breath in my body.

XVIII

It's the beginning of December in the year of our Lord Eleven Hundred and Thirty-Five. Five months and more have passed since Eadwerd and I danced throughout the balmy midsummer night. And I love Ed not a jot less than I ever did. The ha'penny whistle was right. It's never wrong. It revealed the truth about love. So says Sunny. And now he tells us that the whistle is issuing him grave warnings over our king: Henry the First, fourth-born son of the Conqueror. King Henry, who has a lot on his plate. More lands – in Normandy and in England – than most men could dream of. More lampreys on his platter, too, than most men would eat in a lifetime. A veritable surfeit.

He'll raise the first mouthful to his lips.

Delicious, he'll think.

The whistle warns that King Henry should take care. The fate of his three brothers should be a lesson to him. Richard, the Conqueror's second-born son, died young when the two tusks of an enraged wild boar impaled him. William Rufus, the Conqueror's successor as King of England, died when two fingers fired an arrow into his back. Possibly at Henry's behest, though the whistle suspects the church. Robert, Duke of Normandy (eldest and least favoured of the Conqueror's sons) died imprisoned by Henry in Cardiff Castle, having lost the sight of his two eyes. And now Henry himself will raise another lamprey to his two lips.

He's away in Normandy, out of the reach of Sunny's whistle, and so he won't heed the warning.

After a while, Sunny stops playing and slips the pipe into his belt.

'We can't know for certain what the future holds in its hand. The future's grip is tenuous and equivocal. But the whistle tells me that King Henry's about to die, as indeed we all must, one day,' he informs us. 'And mark this. The Conqueror's four sons must account for their actions to the Almighty. As for the rest of us – the living - we'll be brought to our knees. The very gates of hell are about to open. War, anarchy and the wrath of God are about to descend upon this godforsaken island.'

He looks directly towards Ed and then me.

'Mark this, too, Perty, Eadwerd,' he adds. 'Hope and love will be all we have to cling to. So says the whistle.'

*Following Henry the First's death,
owing to "a surfeit of lampreys", in 1135,
the sometimes brutal civil war often referred to as
"The Anarchy" would ravage England
(albeit sporadically, in its latter stages)
until 1153, when Henry's grandson,
Henry the Second, would ascend to the throne.*